Hope Robinson has always been ⌐   but
for many years, his busy life – filled with den⌐   eers
for both himself and his wife, as well as the joys and
responsibilities of raising a daughter and a son – meant his
writing efforts were sporadic and often left him feeling
unsatisfied. During the second COVID-19 lockdown and
winter weather, he decided then was the time to sit down and
see if he could write to his satisfaction. He hopes others will
find as much joy in reading them as he did in crafting them.

For my wife and daughter.

Hope Robinson

A Question and Other Stories

AUSTIN MACAULEY PUBLISHERS™

LONDON • CAMBRIDGE • NEW YORK • SHARJAH

Copyright © Hope Robinson 2024

The right of Hope Robinson to be identified as author of this work has been asserted by the author in accordance with sections 77 and 78 of the Copyright, Designs and Patents Act 1988.

All rights reserved. No part of this publication may be reproduced, stored in a retrieval system, or transmitted in any form or by any means, electronic, mechanical, photocopying, recording, or otherwise, without the prior permission of the publishers.

Any person who commits any unauthorised act in relation to this publication may be liable to criminal prosecution and civil claims for damages.

This is a work of fiction. Names, characters, businesses, places, events, locales, and incidents are either the products of the author's imagination or used in a fictitious manner. Any resemblance to actual persons, living or dead, or actual events is purely coincidental.

A CIP catalogue record for this title is available from the British Library.

ISBN 9781035838684 (Paperback)
ISBN 9781035838691 (ePub e-book)

www.austinmacauley.com

First Published 2024
Austin Macauley Publishers Ltd®
1 Canada Square
Canary Wharf
London
E14 5AA

Table of Contents

A Fresh

The telephone rang. He answered it. "Hi Matt, it's Jason, I've just had a look at the beck. After last night's rain, there is a fresh on. I would like to go down the beck myself, up to the neck in it at the workshop. I've got a gearbox to strip down, an old Ford. Just thought you might like to know." Matt thanked Jason and put the phone down. Jason was a good friend. It had been difficult recently when talking to him. Well, fishing the beck was as good a way as any to pass the time of day on a Saturday.

Fifteen minutes later, Matt was ready to go. He left the house and walked along Newby road towards the beck. People he knew, or were just acquainted with, greeted him. Some, obviously having said 'good morning', quickly moved on. Others, when they spoke to him, had a note of sympathy in their voices. They were aware of his situation. Still, the village had been a good choice when they were looking for somewhere to live. It was only a twenty-minute drive to the office for him. She had worked from home.

At the bottom of the steps from the road bridge, with his rod and reel, Matt tackled up on the bank of the beck. It did not take long; he was well-practised. He looked at the beck. Yes, the rain overnight had increased the water level. Water draining off the hills into streams had not been sufficient to create flood conditions. A 'fresh', the term he had first heard when they had come to live in the Dales. After a dry spell when the water level was low, the conditions now were just right to fish the beck. Tasty morsels for the trout washed down as the water drained. It always caused a trout-feeding frenzy.

After two hours, Matt had fished his way along the bank of the beck and reached the point locally called Quarry Hole. The bank opposite had been quarried in the last century, and the beck slowed as water flowed into a pool area. This was one of Matt's favourite spots. He put his tackle bag down and cast. He reeled in the lure. Spinning was always his preferred method when fishing the beck. A take. Matt played the trout. It soon tired, he reeled it in, and landed it. Another nice native brown trout. Rainbow trout were occasionally caught in the beck; they escaped from a put-and-take fishery established in old gravel workings. Water drained from the workings into the beck. No need to get the priest out of his tackle bag to give the trout the last rites. With practised ease, Matt held the trout, a hand on either side of its gills. With a quick move, the trout ceased trying to wriggle free. Matt put the trout into the bag he had brought for the purpose. There were already seven others in there. Four brace, he thought to himself, if anyone wanted to be snooty about it. Time for a break. Matt took two paces forward, bent down, and washed his hands in the beck. Having dried his hands on a cloth, he decided to have a cigarette. He laid his rod on the grass, his tackle bag by his feet, and sat down on a protruding boulder. Matt exhaled and looked at the cigarette.

Four weeks had passed since he had started smoking again. He had given it up for her when they first met, three years and seven months ago. It was Saturday again. Matt's thoughts returned to the Saturday four weeks prior. On that Saturday morning, everything seemed normal. No rush, a leisurely breakfast in their dressing gowns. Small talk, and she mentioned home service jobs that needed doing. None were a challenge for his DIY skills. As usual, he had cleared up after they finished eating. And, as usual, she got up to go upstairs to shower and dress. He had glanced at the morning paper for five minutes or so and then decided he should shower and dress. Plans could be made for their day afterwards. As he walked into the hall, she was at the foot of the stairs with a suitcase. Dressed to go out, her words echoed in his head again, "I'm leaving you. I'm going away with Glen. He has got a new job as a sales manager near York. I have seen a solicitor; you will probably know her. Divorce documents are being sent to you. The grounds for my divorce from you are my adultery with Glen." Looking back, Matt still could not get over how she had told him. Matter of fact, deadpan. No emotion in evidence at all. She said nothing further, turned, opened the door, picked up the suitcase, walked out, and closed the door behind her. From the lounge window, he had seen her being greeted by Glen at the garden gate. They had kissed before Glen put her suitcase into the boot of his car. They both got into the car and drove away. Matt closed his mind to further thoughts about that Saturday and Sunday. On Monday morning, as he drove to his office, his mind made up; in fact, a shutter had come down regarding her—move on. It would take time, of course. There were still some matters to sort out. The divorce would be, from what he had been told, a rubber-stamp job, her admission of adultery with a third party guaranteeing that.

Matt scanned the pool. Subtle movement in the slow-flowing water told him trout were feeding. One rose—a splash, a fly rise. He looked at his watch; two and a half hours had passed since he had commenced fishing. Time to have a snack lunch. Matt got a lunch box and a flask out of his tackle bag. As he took the lid off the box, he thought about his evening meal. Yes, trout rolled in oats with a Caesar salad. He had a couple of trout in the freezer. Any others, he would give to his neighbours. Readily accepted, gutted, ready to cook. Matt ate his chicken salad sandwich. He had taken a whole chicken out of the freezer, timed to be cooked when he got home from the office. Now it was too much for one meal. A chicken risotto tomorrow, Sunday. Sufficient for two. He needed no help in the kitchen, thanks to his mum. Matt poured coffee from his flask. His mum—she would have to be told. It was his turn to call last Sunday; "Everything is fine," he had said when asked. He decided to finish early next Friday and drive down to Taunton, staying until Sunday. It would be better to tell his mum face-to-face that she had left him, rather than on the telephone.

Matt ate his second sandwich and looked around—lovely countryside, peaceful and quiet. Another man fishing some distance away. Apart from him, there was no one else around. He would continue to live in the village; he enjoyed living there. Like many in the Dales, it was mainly stone-built. He knew his neighbours and others like his friend Jason would have known what she and Glen were up to. For him, there had been no indication of what was going on. Her working from home and Glen working as a sales rep for an agricultural supplier gave them numerous opportunities to be together. Matt poured the last of his coffee from the flask into his cup.

Jason who he had got to know well, would not, of course, have said a word. Jason serviced his car, and their shared interest in angling had brought them together. On Friday evening at the pub, the Mitre, both of them sat with Jason and his wife Pat. No indication. Glen had paused when he arrived, exchanged pleasantries, and then joined his two friends whom he regularly drank with. Not a hint. Matt drank the last of his coffee, put the cup back on the flask, and with his sandwich box, returned to his tackle bag. As a trout rose in the pool, the memory of that Friday when they had returned from the pub came back to him. She had come to him, as she often did, as they undressed, and what followed between them contradicted her words on Saturday morning. He had not slept in that bed since. When was the last time she and Glen lay on it, having sex? He sat for two minutes; trout rose and birds flew close to the water. A fly hatch was rising.

"Hello, my dearest darling Matthew. When you were not at home, I thought I would find you down the beck," her voice echoed. Matt turned, and there she stood. Auburn hair down to her shoulders, a smile on her lips. The light coat she wore when she left was open, revealing a blouse and skirt. The blouse was sufficiently unbuttoned to show cleavage. She continued, "I left Glen this morning. I realised over the past week, my dearest, that it is you whom I truly love. Please, Matthew darling, forgive me for my indiscretion. We can start afresh; our lives will bed down again." As she spoke those words, her smile still there, her head tilted a little to the left, and her eyelids slightly closed. She continued, "We still have our future ahead of us." Seconds passed. Matt deliberately took a packet of cigarettes out of his pocket and selected one. He put the packet back into his pocket and lit the cigarette.

"A fresh start? The only 'fresh' I'm interested in today is the one on the beck. As for 'bedding down' you have made a bed for yourself, and as far as I am concerned, you can lie in it. As for the future, I've more or less dealt with divorce matters. The solicitor you consulted and paid a fee to, I do know her. We have worked very well together several times. I've lunched and spent two evenings with her last week. Tomorrow she will join me for the day. Sooner or later, I hope she will marry me. With Lana, all being well, I will start afresh."

An Affair?

Thoughts

The film on TV ended as I thought it would. I switched the TV off. Janine is not a big fan of films. Moira loves a good film. I sat and pondered the day's events. A pleasant morning was spent reading the Sunday newspapers with Janine. Moira prefers to read the news on her phone. We had a nice lunch— roast beef with all the trimmings. Moira is a vegetarian. We took a walk in the park with Janine, and a happy little girl with her teddy bear in her pushchair. It was a pleasant afternoon. Near the pond, after we finished feeding the ducks, Moira jogged towards us. Janine prefers walking for exercise. We chatted, and Moira informed us that our little boy was with his grandparents for the afternoon. I suggested having coffee. We sat with coffee and cakes at the café near the park entrance. The topic of holidays came up. Janine and Moira agreed on the same villa in Spain as last year—a nice garden and a safe pool for the children, with restaurants nearby where you can get steak. Moira jokingly said—I said I had no problem cooking my own steak when needed. The possibility of both families living in the same house was mentioned. "Not yet," Janine said, given the state of the housing market. I agreed and shared of what I knew and could reveal about potential interest rate movements.

As we talked, I noticed again how the differences in opinion and approach to life between Janine and Moira blended and merged, to the point where the distinctions between them had little meaning or impact when they were in each other's company. They had grown up together—same school, similar examination results, university, and degree. They shared interests in clothes, makeup, shoes, and a love of playing tennis and other activities. After graduation, they both went their separate ways, both of them qualifying as solicitors. They led busy lives, exchanging birthday and Christmas cards and phone calls to stay in touch, occasionally meeting up.

Time for bed. I switch off the electric fire; the flame effect makes it a focal point in the lounge. Moira says laying a real fire is not much of a chore. There are things to do. I check that the kitchen door is locked. No need to check with Moira; the door is always locked at five on an autumn evening. I feed Mini puss cat. Moira likes cats but prefers dogs, especially Rusty, her Yorkshire terrier. Now, make sure all the downstairs lights are switched off. Moira says if a light is not needed, don't leave it switched on. The house will stay warm overnight; the boiler will activate if the temperature drops below freezing. Moira says all you need is each other and a good quality duvet to keep warm at night. Now, upstairs, the first thing to do is check on a little lady. A curly-haired head with her teddy bear, fast asleep. In the bathroom, there's an electric toothbrush. Moira says we can supply all the energy needed to clean our teeth. I go into the bedroom; Janine looks up and smiles, turns a page, and continues to read. Moira prefers to sit downstairs by the side of a log fire to read at this time of year. I get into bed and lie on my side, looking at my lovely Janine reading. She will read to the end of a chapter before using a bookmark to note the page she has reached. Moira always folds the corner of the page down to do the same thing. With the page marked and the bedside light switched off, Janine moves close to me. She puts her arm over my chest and slowly moves her hand down over my stomach and onto my hip. We kiss. Her hand moves down to my thigh. I wait in anticipation; I know what Janine will do next. I move my hand from her breast down her side until I reach her thigh. I kiss her forehead, her cheeks and, her lips. What unfolds next is always a joy, a delight. My love for Janine is all-consuming. No thoughts of Moira.

Later, I lie with my arms around Janine, and she moves as close to me as she can and goes to sleep. I think back to the evening I stood outside the bank at six and waited for Janine and Moira on Thread-needle Street. The two women I loved so deeply. I have never been able to put a finger on how my love for both of them differed in any significant way. Janine and Moira were seen on different evenings during the week. I saw Janine on Saturday and Moira on Sunday, each of them saying they loved me. I had told them both that they were the loves of my life. I knew either of them would say yes to spend the rest of their lives with me. I could no longer put off telling them that I had been seeing them both—a dilemma for me.

I saw Janine cross the street as Moira reached the corner. They greeted each other with a hug and stood chatting. They walked together down Thread-needle Street, chatting and smiling. It was then that I realised they were good friends who probably had not seen each other for some time—catching up. They walked towards me, and as they approached, both of them smiled and held out a hand to me. I took hold of both of their hands. They looked at me and then at each other and back to me, a look of surprise on their faces. Before they could speak, I told them both that I had to decide to tell one of them that I had met someone else. I explained that I was unable to decide and that I wanted to be with them both. I had then said that if they both wished to walk away from me now, I would understand. I mentioned that I would continue thinking of them both for the rest of my life, as no other woman could take their place.

Janine stirred in her sleep and murmured something. This week with Janine and our daughter, thoughts of Moira. Next week with Moira and our son, thoughts of Janine.

Ten Years Later

Winnie put her paintbrush down and looked at a photograph alongside her painting. Animal portraits were not something she had undertaken often. She smiled, content that her work and the image on the photograph coincided. The cat's expression and fur colour she had captured to her satisfaction, through a little more work on the ears was needed. It was a neighbour's cat that had often wandered through the garden, now in cat heaven. If all went well, her neighbour Mrs Grenly, who had grieved for a week over her cat, would be happy with the portrait. She was only making some finishing touches now. Enough was enough; the day, as forecast, was clouding over. Better light was needed to continue. Winnie locked her studio door and walked down the garden path to the house. Plan A, partially completed. Plan B, start by clearing up in the kitchen.

Winnie rung out the dishcloth and pulled the plug out in the kitchen sink, allowing the soapy water to drain away. Winnie smiled, looking forward to a day to herself—a lady of leisure. The benefits of supply teaching. She could choose when and where she worked, and the demand for her services was always there. Three hours with 1D at the Convent School? As much as she enjoyed teaching, it had not appealed to her. Mary would take it. Since her husband's accident, his left hand injured by the machine he worked on, Mary needed the money. Winnie liked Mary and passed work to her from time to time in order to give Mary the chance to supplement her income.

Winnie looked at the kitchen clock, 9:05—more than enough time to get to the station and catch the 10 o'clock train. It was a warm day; Winnie took a light coat in case it turned cold or rained later. She locked the front door and walked on the stepping stones set in the lawn to get to her car. Winnie smiled as she started her new car, a top-of-the-range Volkswagen E-Up. Yes, some would say it was expensive, priced at just over twenty-two thousand pounds. However, it was ideal for what Winnie needed; she had liked the car straightaway on a test drive.

Winnie parked her car at the station, picked up her coat, and took a carrier bag from the back seat. She locked her car and walked towards the station. With her ticket bought, Winnie stood on the platform and looked at her watch—four minutes before the train was due. There was a station announcement about a ten-minute delay. The train was running late. Paul had told her some time ago that delays in the morning were becoming more frequent. He now left for the station earlier to catch the 7:15 train rather than the 7:45, so he could get to the office on time.

On the train, Winnie placed her coat and the carrier bag on the luggage rack. Her phone in her handbag buzzed as she sat down. It was a text from Mary, saying thanks for giving her name for the work at the Convent school. The carrier bag shifted on the rack, triggering a memory of why it was there. Winnie thought about the previous Sunday—the afternoon spent at their daughter's new house. Paul had helped Lorraine's husband, Michael, put up a curtain rail and shelves. In the carrier bag was a dress that Lorraine had bought and then decided to return. Winnie had volunteered to take it back to M&S., Lorraine was still at work, and Winnie and Paul's grandchild was still six months away from being born. Winnie smiled to herself at the thought and relaxed in her seat.

The train arrived at Castle Street station, slowed and came to a stop. Winnie got off and walked to the exit, the station being familiar to her. For four years, she had commuted here after she and Paul got married. Winnie had continued to teach at the Girls High School full-time, leaving when she was pregnant with Lorraine. As she walked down the slope from the station, an art exhibition was advertised on a notice board. Local artists and children's paintings were on display. The exhibition was at the City Art Gallery. Winnie was interested. She held an arts degree and had specialised in drawing and painting. While her teaching subject was art, she often found herself teaching English and other subjects at an introductory level. She enjoyed the variety.

With the dress returned and a refund obtained, Winnie window-shopped and browsed the counters in department stores. She enjoyed looking around the shops, though Paul hated it. Winnie bought a blouse and a pair of trousers from a charity shop. Time was her own, and Winnie was happy and content with life. The city hall clock struck two, and Winnie decided to go to the art exhibition. The art gallery was only a four-to-five-minutes-walk away. Before visiting the exhibition, she would have a snack lunch and a drink at the café near the gallery.

As Winnie waited to cross the road to go to the café, she was shocked. Coming out of the café was Paul, with a woman. They walked along the pavement, heads close together, and stopped near the crossing by the steps of the art gallery. The woman put her hand on Paul's arm, and he moved closer to her. The crossing light changed to green, people stepped forward, but Winnie stepped back and continued to watch her husband and the woman standing close together, deep in conversation. They walked towards the crossing. Winnie quickly stepped into a shop doorway, noticing a sign on the door that said 'Closed for lunch'. As Paul and the woman crossed the road, Winnie could see that she was younger than her. The woman had a good figure and was well-dressed in a skirt and matching jacket. She wore high-heeled shoes in the same light yellow shade as her skirt and jacket. Her hair was shoulder-length and raven black. Paul and the woman crossed the road, turning left, walking a few paces before stopping. Again their heads were close together, and the woman whispered something in Paul's ear. He smiled and replied. They continued walking, and the woman linked her arm with Paul's. Winnie knew that the office block where Paul worked was only minutes away. Winnie stood in the shop doorway, her once happy frame of mind gone, replaced by a sick feeling in her stomach. Her darling husband was involved with another woman.

Winnie looked at herself in the shop window. She was wearing a skirt and a blouse that she often wore when teaching, bought in a charity shop. Her flat-heeled shoes and the light coat she had on had been bought a number of years ago. Winnie could not imagine walking in the high-heeled shoes that the woman wore. Her legs seemed more elegant than the ones she saw in the shop window, her own. Her hair was in the short style that she had always preferred—not down to her shoulders, and it did not swirl when she moved her head.

Lunch and the art exhibition were forgotten. All Winnie wanted was to go home. She waved down a taxi and got in, instructing the driver to go to 'Castle Street station'. The taxi pulled out into the traffic. She had left the items she had bought in a carrier bag still in the shop doorway. As she sat in the taxi, all her feelings of disbelief, shock and anger at what she'd seen resurfaced. Her darling Paul was in intimate contact with a younger woman. Winnie sobbed, and tears ran down her cheeks. He was obviously involved with her. How far had this gone? The tissue she had with her was soon soaked with her tears. The taxi driver, slowing to let a bus pull out, glanced in his mirror. The taxi slowed again and stopped at traffic lights. The driver took a clean handkerchief out of his pocket and passed it to Winnie through the gap in the plastic screen, saying, "Here you are, love." Winnie said, "Thanks." Nothing more was said.

The taxi pulled into the taxi rank at Castle Street station, "That's £8.20, love," the driver said. Winnie took a ten-pound note out of her purse and gave it to the driver, saying, "Keep the change." She ran up the slope and into the station, without having to think, she crossed the bridge to platform two.

Five minutes later, a train pulled in, and Winnie got on. There were not many passengers at that time of the day. She sat down, still crying and seeing Paul and the woman close together in her mind's eye. A man looked at her, said something to his wife, and then went back to reading his newspaper. Thoughts raced through Winnie's brain—Paul was having an affair. The woman was young and good-looking. Now it was obvious to Winnie why, over the past months, Paul had often been late coming home from work. Last night, he had been over two hours late. Winnie knew the usual arrival time of the train Paul normally caught. She always prepared their evening meal for around seven o'clock, Paul's regular train arrived at 6:30. When she heard the sound of Paul's car in the driveway, she would take their meal and warm plates out of the oven. It was a nice routine—Paul was home.

The journey, one she knew so well, seemed to last longer than she could ever remember. Winnie left the station and ran to her car, got in, and still crying, drove home. She had a near miss with a delivery van at the traffic lights the sound of a horn and the driver waving his fist. She parked the car in its usual place, a carport next to the garage. Mrs Nettleton, a neighbour who lived opposite, waved to her. Winnie waved back, walked to the front door, and quickly went into the house. The last thing she wanted was a conversation with Mrs Nettleton about gardens or the price of fish and milk.

Time passed. Winnie sat on the settee in the lounge, her mind in a whirl. At five o'clock, Winnie went into the kitchen and started to prepare an evening meal: rib-eye steak, new potatoes, tomatoes, mushrooms, and broccoli. She had bought all the ingredients yesterday on her way home from Grove Academy. By 8 o'clock, there was still no sign of Paul. Winnie served her own meal and tried to eat, but it was no use. At 8:30, she got up from the table and in the kitchen, she scraped over half of her plate of food into the kitchen bin. Winnie stood with the plate in her hand and wept. Where was Paul? By 9:30, there was still no sign of him. His meal remained in the oven. At 11:00, he still hadn't returned. Where was he? No more trains were running tonight. Paul was not coming home. Winnie tried Paul's phone again, but as before, it was not available. Winnie cried again, trying to convince herself that her thoughts weren't true. Paul was with that young woman. Were they in a hotel room or at her apartment?

In the kitchen, Winnie switched off the oven, leaving Paul's meal dried out. In the lounge, she switched off the lights and the TV—she had not watched it. She left the hall light on and went upstairs. For the first time ever, Winnie did not bother to wash or clean her teeth. In the bedroom, she undressed and put her nightdress on, then got into bed. Tears flowed once again. Paul was not going to be in bed with her tonight. Would he ever be again? Winnie buried her head in her pillow and wept uncontrollably. Time passed slowly, and Winnie found it impossible to sleep. She looked at the bedside clock—midnight. She sobbed again and said aloud, "Paul, please don't leave me. I love you, Paul." Thoughts raced through her mind—had he taken ill? An accident? No, there had been no phone call from Paul or anyone else. He always had his phone, driving license, and credit and debit cards on him. If something had happened to him, someone would have phoned. No, Paul was with that young woman. Winnie felt certain of it. She turned her pillow over and buried her head in it, and again, her tears flowed.

Winnie did not hear Paul's car on the drive, or the front door open. Paul breathed a sigh of relief as he quietly closed the door, knowing Winnie would be in bed. He took off his jacket and waistcoat, placing them over the back of a chair in the hall. Then, he took off his shoes and put them under the chair. In the lounge, he put his phone on to charge. Quietly in his stocking feet, Paul climbed the stairs with the intention of quickly washing and cleaning his teeth. At the top of the stairs, he paused, hearing a sound. He realised Winnie was crying. He dashed into the bedroom, asking urgently, "Winnie, has something happened? It's not Lorraine and the baby? Please, don't say that." Paul switched on the bedroom light as Winnie replied, "No, Paul, nothing like that." "My darling Winnie, tell me, please, what is the matter?" "I saw you today, Paul, with a younger woman—very nice-looking, and you seemed very involved with her." Paul looked at Winnie and smiled. "You've got the wrong end of the stick, darling. Put on your dressing gown and slippers and come downstairs. I will tell you about her. I will put the kettle on, and we will have a mug of coffee and brandy."

Winnie sat on the settee as Paul came in from the kitchen. "Here we are, coffee. I will get the brandy, and then you can tell me what happened." Moments later, Paul sat down and placed two glasses of brandy on the coffee table. Winnie looked at Paul, and he asked, "What happened, Winnie?" She told him, "I returned a dress for Lorraine and looked around the shops. I decided to go to the art gallery to see an exhibition. I saw you and her, whoever she is, coming out of the café where I intended to have lunch. She's young, lovely-looking, with nice hair, and very well-dressed. Both of you close together, happy and smiling. I thought I had lost you, Paul. I looked at myself in a shop window and realised I was what I'd been since university when we first met. Someone who has never been bothered about clothes and appearance. Typical of many art teachers, well, not all." "Winnie, dearest, that was you when we first met and I bought you a drink in the union bar. Remember, fresher's week for you? I was on my final year. You were typical of many art students, with a style of dress all your own. Unlike many of those studying with me and my friends in the law department—string of pearls types, most of them. But, like you say about art teachers, not all of them. I loved you from that first drink. You always play your part, if a long dress for you and a bow tie for me is required. Otherwise, you are who you are, and that's fine by me. I still love you, Winnie, for being you in every respect. The lady you saw me with is called Janine. I will tell you about her. Janine has worked with me for the last year or so. My working world since I became a senior member of the firm is more pressurised and stressful than in the past. Clients, barristers, and others to meet and discuss cases with. And yes, court appearances for me, of course. Its deadlines all the time. As you know, we are not everyday solicitors. Janine holds a senior position in the firm and is excellent—a high flier. She earned a first class in law at Cambridge and qualifying as a solicitor on the first attempt. Yours truly, a 2:2 and qualifying on the second attempt. I took it from there, as you know. Janine and I complement each other. We help each other and can deal with problems together much more easily than we can with others in the office. Janine is always more up-to-date than me; I have to look up the latest cases and statutes. The last thing I want to do is pick up the New Law Journal and read it in my spare time. Janine always has a copy of the Cambridge Law Journal available. On the other hand, being longer in the tooth, I know my way around the system and know more people than Janine does. As I said, we complement each other. Janine did have career breaks due to having children and a domestic situation. Yes, I have been coming home later than previously; work is piling up and becoming more complicated."

"Tonight I should have been home at the usual time. A derailment, a goods train on a bridge—it created chaos. I was on the platform with Joe, who I often travel with. My phone needed charging, Joe had left his phone at the office. The two pay phones on the station were vandalised. The buffet bar was closed, so we just stood on the platform and waited. Announcements kept saying a train would arrive. One did eventually. At the station, Joe's wife was there to meet him; she always drops him at the station and picks him up. Nina, Joe's wife, said there had been an announcement on the local TV news. All explained, Winnie darling?"

"Yes and no, Paul. She touched and linked her arm in yours and your heads were close together when you were speaking to each other. It did not look to me as though you and Janine were simply colleagues out to lunch. It looked to me very much as though you were involved with her." Paul sat back and said nothing for a moment. "Winnie, you are wrong about an affair. I have only touched Janine's hand once, and that was when we shook hands when we were introduced. Yes, she does link her arm in mine. It's the same with other men she knows and trusts. Her hand on my arm is quite a regular thing. She does not mean anything by it in the way that you are thinking. Now, I'm not a psychoanalyst, but, yes, I suppose we have what you might call a strong friendship. We are very close, as I've said, and we share our work and our problems. It's not as I have said, Winnie, what you are thinking in any shape or form. I love you, I always have. Please believe me, Winnie. Think of last weekend, Saturday afternoon and Saturday night." "Yes, Paul it was lovely. You were more relaxed than you have been for quite some time. If there is so much stress now for you, can't you stand back a little?" "In two years, Winnie, I hope to retire, earlier than originally planned. Think about our situation—this house with its nice gardens and, yes, your studio near the Orchard. We both love it here, and we have no wish to move. Your car—we could have bought the basic model ten grand cheaper. Mine, a Merc 350 E, not much change out of fifty-five thousand pounds. Money behind us in the bank and in a range of investments. The holidays we have had and more to come, all being well. Another two years to consolidate our situation, that's what I need. It's actually reached the point where I almost hate the bloody job. It pays a hell of a lot of cash though. Your day-to-day situation, teaching part-time. None of the stress that full-time teaching involves. You can pick and choose; we don't need the money. You also have plenty of time to spend a number of hours every day in your studio. You enjoy your life as it is, and that's fine by me. Some problems I've discussed with Janine that I should have mentioned to you. But, I have never brought the office home. Winnie, you know that. You have no more interest in law than I can appreciate the use of colour on a sunny or a rainy day with regard to landscapes." Moments passed, nothing was said.

"You say that Janine talks about her worries and problems to you, as you do to her. Will you tell me more about her?" "All right Winnie, here goes. Janine has two children, a girl and a boy. Her friend Moira has three, a girl and two boys. They live in the same house. About a year after Moira's daughter, her third child, was born, she was seriously injured by a hit-and-run driver. Moira was working part-time; like Janine, she is a qualified solicitor. It has taken time for Moira to walk again. She can now, with the aid of a crutch, Janine told me. Janine had just over a year's career break, five children to consider. Janine feels she has a responsibility to support her friend and, of course, their children. Now, what I have never got my head around is this. All five children have the same father; he is their daddy on a day-to-day basis. He is very high up in banking, Janine has never said quite what. She did say he has appeared on TV, News night three times. The 'no one else available' situation. Janine refers to him as her husband. I presume Moira does as well. I have never met Moira or their husband. Another thing that I found strange is this. The children refer to Janine as 'Mummy J' and to Moira as 'Mummy M'. So it's complicated. But I will repeat again, there is not anything going on between Janine and me whatsoever." Paul sighed, minutes past, nothing said.

Paul sat forward, picked up his glass of brandy, and drank it. "Winnie dearest, let's sort this out. I have got to go back into the office tomorrow morning, you know how much I hate having to do that. Saturday ruined. Janine will be there. Come with me. You can go to the art exhibition at the gallery in the morning, and Janine and I will meet you for lunch. The café near the gallery is a good place to meet. Janine will reassure you what you are thinking is wrong." "Paul, I don't know if that's a good idea or not." "Winnie, I have talked to Janine about you from time to time, so she does know of you. My phone should be charged sufficiently now; I will send Janine a text. Janine always checks her phone first thing in the morning before she gets up. She will know you are coming with me." Paul got up, walked to the sideboard, and picked up his phone. Winnie watched him, with thoughts in her head. "He's talked to Janine about me, but I have never heard him mention her name once. He knows when she checks her phone. I don't think he has a clue when I check mine." Winnie was not reassured. The day's events and what Paul had said to her in her mind compounding the situation. She felt just left out after what Paul had told her about Janine. It was though Paul was living two lives: one with her and another with Janine.

Upstairs, Winnie washed and cleaned her teeth, looking at herself in the bathroom mirror. Her thoughts raced, "I'm not plain, but Janine, with her looks and figure, could easily be on the front page of Vogue. Her hair is styled regularly, while I have only had minor trims since the day Paul and I got married. From what I saw today and from what Paul said, Janine is a big part of his life, and I have been totally excluded from it. How can I compete with her?" Doubts filled her mind, "Am I doing the right thing by going to meet her tomorrow?" Winnie hurriedly returned down the landing. She quickly got into bed, and lay on her left side to face away from Paul. As she lay there, she heard Paul come upstairs and head to the bathroom, the faint sound of running water reaching her ears. In the bedroom, Paul undressed, got into bed, and switched off the light. Paul had never worn pyjamas. He moved close to Winnie and put his arm around her. "I love you, Winnie," He whispered. The day had been long, and soon Paul drifted off to sleep. However, Winnie remained awake, her mind swirling with thoughts. Eventually, the weight of the day caught up with her, and she succumbed to sleep.

Winnie woke up at six in the morning, she got up, leaving Paul still sleeping. She showered and washed her hair before looking at herself in the wardrobe mirror. At first, she put on a dress that she had occasionally worn for receptions at Paul's office. However, she quickly changed her mind, deciding not to go out of her way to impress. "Damn dressing up, I will just be myself, I will wear what I would to go to a school to teach," She thought. Satisfied with that thought, she changed and smiled as she looked at herself in the mirror. A blouse, cardigan, and a long skirt that she had worn often. Looking at her reflection, she said aloud, "This is me." "It's you, Winnie, as always. Fine by me. I will be in a suit, collar, and tie as usual." Paul had woken up and watched her as she dressed. He got out of bed, took Winnie in his arms, and kissed her. "I love you, Winnie. Now, I'm off for a shower."

Saturday morning, no problem parking at the station. A first-class ticket for her; Paul travelling on his season-ticket. Paul normally only had a mug of tea before leaving home—a fried breakfast on the train covered by his season-ticket. This morning he ate cereal, toast, and marmalade, washed down with a mug of tea. Winnie had eaten very little: half a slice of buttered toast with a cup of tea. The train slowly came into the station; as it stopped, Winnie was tempted to ask Paul for his car keys so she could drive home. Doors opened, people got out, and Paul stood back. Winnie got on the train, followed by Paul. Saturday morning, limited first-class service: drinks, biscuits, and other snacks. Winnie drank her coffee but had to force herself to eat a packet of three ginger biscuits. Paul finished his coffee and put his cup down. "Something I was going to tell you last night, Winnie, if I had arrived home on time. Janine has a client, an art dealer. He was with Janine in her office yesterday morning. He looked at your seascape in Janine's office. It's the one with the ruined castle on a cliff at sunset. He told Janine he would give her £1,000 for it. Janine said it was not for sale and told him that her colleague's wife had painted the picture. Janine introduced me to him, and he looked at your painting of the Martello tower in my office and the other two landscapes you painted. He looked at them through the glass doors of my partner's offices. He offered me £2,000 for the Martello tower. You only ever, as you know, sign your paintings 'Winnie'. I confirmed you were my wife and an art teacher. He gave me a card and asked me to ask you to get in touch with him. The card is in my wallet; I will give it to you later. Your decision, of course. But, if you think about it, all the paintings you have in your studio and in the spare bedrooms, he could be interested in them. This chap's gallery is in Knightsbridge, a clientele with money. He talked about your titles, 'At Sunset' and 'Midday', and how you had captured the time of day, shade, that sort of thing. As you know, it's all a closed shop to me. Janine followed what he was saying; it seems she did an art course at Cambridge when she was studying law. Think about it, Winnie, I will obviously leave it to you." What Paul had said interested Winnie; yes, others she knew that taught did sell their work from time to time. She had never really thought about trying to sell her paintings on a commercial basis.

Winnie's thoughts returned to why she was on the train, to meet Janine. What will she say to me about Paul? Did she really want to know? Should she bother, or, despite what Paul might say, catch the next train home? She could go to Lorraine's, talk to her, and ask if she could stay there for a few days to think things over? No, not fair to Lorraine, upsetting her now by telling her about her dad and Janine. The train moved slowly into a tunnel, as Winnie and Paul knew it would. It emerged alongside platform one, Castle Street station. The train stopped and the doors opened. Winnie got up, followed by Paul. Outside the station, it was Saturday, so there was no waiting for a taxi.

The taxi stopped outside the office block where Paul worked. It was an imposing building, designed to make an impression. Winnie had been there before, accompanying Paul to receptions and events, dressed as he had described. She would play the role of a middle-class wife who taught and painted for her own enjoyment. These events, like the annual dinner dance, were not her cup of tea. There were often people with inflated opinions of themselves, and where they thought they should be in life, and an attitude of disregard for others. These were exceptions, though. However, she was always relieved when it was time to go home. Winnie's background, school, and aspects of her mum and dad's social life she had been involved in, equipped her to play the part when she wished to. She wondered if Janine had been at the last social gathering. If so, she would have recognised her when she saw Janine yesterday. Winnie remembered that she had skipped the last reception due to a head cold. It seemed that Paul had an uncanny ability to avoid colds. After getting out of the taxi, Paul turned to her and said, "See you at about twelve, Winnie."

"Art gallery, please," Winnie instructed the driver.

On the opposite side of the street from the art gallery, the taxi stopped. Winnie paid the fare and got out of the taxi. She

33

was outside the shop where she had watched Paul and Janine from the doorway the day before. It sold women's and children's clothes. She remembered leaving her carrier bag here. Winnie went into the shop as a little girl and her mother left, Winnie approached an assistant and inquired about her lost carrier bag. Fortunately, they had found it. Winnie showed the assistant her receipts, and the carrier bag was handed back to her. Winnie looked at coats on display, duffel coats. "They are in fashion, madam," she was told. One of the coats was in a mustard colour, obviously new. The one next to it in navy blue looked worn. A label on the coat stated, "Prepared to look authentic for you!" Similar to denim, Winnie thought, faded and tears in jeans to make them look worn. Winnie's dad had a duffel coat he had worn when he was in the Navy, worn by him now when walking with her mum and their spaniel, Polly. Winnie left the shop wearing the navy blue duffel coat with her carrier bag. The light coat she had brought with her was in the carrier bag.

Winnie finished her cup of coffee and watched people passing by. She had chosen an outside table at the café. She had smoked two cigarettes since she sat down. She toyed with the idea of phoning Paul and telling him she was going to go home. The art exhibition had taken her mind off why she was there. Appreciation and criticism as she looked at the various paintings in her mind and in conversation. An art teacher she knew, Mrs Bloxham, was there with her husband. "Another coffee, madam?" "Later, please. I will be joined by two other people." The waitress walked away. Two other people, not my husband and a colleague, she thought. Yesterday, Paul and Janine together looked like two other people who had nothing to do with her. Would they today?

Winnie sighed and looked at her watch, nearly 12 o'clock. She looked to her left towards the crossing, where Paul and Janine were waiting to cross. As yesterday, they were close together, with Janine's arm linked in Paul's. Paul said something to Janine. Janine smiled and replied. They appeared to Winnie as a very happy couple. An older man enjoying time with his young wife. Winnie just wanted to get up and leave. But she remained seated. The crossing light changed, And Paul and Janine crossed the road along with other people. They turned to their left and walked towards the café where Winnie was sitting. Janine looked very smartly dressed in a black two-piece skirt and jacket. She wore black high-heeled shoes and black stockings. Elegant, poised, and confident. The sun glistened on a necklace adorned with diamonds. In contrast, Winnie wore a necklace made of seashells and small pebbles with holes drilled in them— something she often wore when teaching.

Paul and Janine walked over to the table where Winnie was seated. Paul pulled out a chair for Janine, and she sat down. "Winnie, dear, this is Janine," Paul introduced. Janine smiled and said, "Hello Winnie, nice to meet you. Paul has often talked about you." Taking this on board on an everyday basis would not have concerned Winnie. Her husband talking to Janine about her, never in turn mentioning Janine at home. Paul looked inside the café and said, "They seem busy today, I will go and order coffee; we can decide on food later."

"We have time to talk, Winnie. Paul's text said you thought we are having an affair. Please believe me, Winnie, it is just not true." Janine paused and took a packet of cigarettes out of her shoulder bag. Winnie noticed the maker's name, Gucci. What else? Her shoulder bag bought cheap from a market stall. Janine offered Winnie a cigarette as she started to speak again, "Paul and I have what you might say a close friendship that has come about due to our mutual professional interests. We get on very well together, we complement each other," Janine said as she put a cigarette in a cigarette holder. Winnie had only ever seen one in films and TV programmes. Janine continued, "We work so well together, and yes, we have discussed aspects of our lives, worries, and aspirations that I should probably have discussed with my husband, and Paul with you. It's just happened this way over time. We always talk for twenty minutes or so in the morning; we both arrive early." Janine's words felt like a knife point in Winnie's stomach. So much for Paul catching an earlier train due to delays. Janine continued, "Please believe me, Winnie, in a physical sense, there has never been any contact between us. Yes, we have become very dependent on each other. I know Paul loves you. He often talks about you and says you have never conformed to what other people think of as the fashion of the day, and that, in itself, means to him you are exceptional. He loves that about you. He told me you only conform when you feel that you should for him from time to time. The reason we have not met at office social functions, by the way, is because I always put our children's interest first. Paul said he had told you about Moira and our husband—unusual, yes, but it works for us." Her manner and the tone of Janine's voice as she talked gave Winnie the impression she was being talked down to. Very middle class. Winnie was not impressed.

Paul returned and sat down, saying, "Coffee will be here in a minute or two." Janine offered Paul a cigarette, he accepted. Janine got a lighter out of her bag—a Janta, Winnie had seen it recently featured in a Sunday paper magazine, reduced to £450. Winnie often looked at products featured with regard to design, although she had no intention of purchasing them. Her lighter cost 70p from the newsagent. Winnie glanced at Janine's hand as a light was offered to her. Slim fingers, manicured nails, polished. Winnie then looked at her own right hand, her nails trimmed short so as not to interfere when delicate brush strokes were required. Paint and charcoal on her hands never bothered her. She used only soap and water, nothing else. Janine, no doubt, used an expensive hand cream. In the bathroom cabinet at home, there was a tube of hand cream given to Winnie by a garden centre she had designed a layout for. She had never used it.

Cigarettes lit, Janine asked, "Please tell us about the exhibition at the gallery, Winnie. There's a reason why I am interested." Winnie proceeded to give her opinion, showing Janine coloured photographs in a brochure. She commented on perspective, use of colour, and the potential for differing opinions. Janine clearly followed what she was saying and added her own comments, her background in the art course she had taken at Cambridge evident in her insights. Paul remained silent. Winnie watched him as she and Janine talked, noticing that his eyes were mostly on Janine. He only occasionally glanced at her. Coffee was served. Winnie continued to discuss her perspective, also sharing her thoughts on the children's exhibition from her point of view as an art teacher. "The reason I asked you, Winnie, is because our eldest, Natasha, my daughter, is very talented. The art teacher at the prep school our children attend suggested that extra lessons might be beneficial. What do you think?" Winnie paused for a moment, wondering if she was being asked for her opinion to make her feel important. Again, a hint of condescension in Janine's voice? If there was, let it go, Winnie answered, "Yes, Janine, if your daughter enjoys art and develops her ability, it'll be beneficial for her enjoyment now and in the future." "Thank you, Winnie. I will go ahead and arrange the extra lessons. There will be a fee, of course; it's a prep school. No doubt you have your own opinions about public school and state school education." Why had she asked that while smiling? An attempt to elicit an anti-public school viewpoint? "Yes, Janine, I have an opinion, but not for the reasons you are probably thinking. I have given extra lessons from time to time, quite simply because pupils have been interested, with no fee involved." Winnie did not enlighten Janine further. She had attended a private girls' school from the age of 12 to 18, leaving as soon as she could after taking her A-levels in Art, Latin, Maths, and English Literature. Winnie Angela Thorpe was a school rebel, often in detention for refusing to behave in a ladylike manner as the school expected. The other girls, of course, complied, soaking up the school's ethos. Only the threat of expulsion, the result of head-butting Susan Grace Hornsby, the star of the upper sixth hockey team, due to her amorous advances in the dormitory, made Winnie toe the line—to a point. Expulsion would have upset her mum. The last thing Winnie wanted for Lorraine was to go through the same experience she had tolerated. Paul had suggested a private education would provide their daughter with advantages in life. Winnie had cut him short when he brought it up.

Janine smiled, "Our children, Moira, and our husband have gone to see the children's exhibition. I hope you don't mind; they are going to join us for lunch." "No problem, Janine." The last thing Winnie wanted was to be joined by others. All the time she had been in the company of Janine and Paul, they often glanced at each other and smiled. Paul had moved closer to Janine than he had been when he first sat down. Nothing going on between them? There was something, it stood out a mile. Again, Winnie just wanted to get up and walk away. Any excuse would do. Paul could make of it what he wanted as far as Winnie was concerned. She looked to her left, intending to get up. Winnie could see five children walking towards the café, the older two walking in front followed by three others. Behind them was a tall man, well-dressed, and a lady holding onto his arm, walking with the aid of a crutch. Moira. She, like Janine, wore black, a trouser suit. Also tall with raven black hair.

Janine and Paul were looking at each other, and something was said that Winnie did not quite hear. As the group drew nearer, Winnie looked again at the man—Janine and Moira's husband, the father of their children. He was dressed in a Harris Tweed jacket and corduroy trousers, giving him the appearance of a gentleman out for a stroll in the country. At his neck, a cravat—a style approach Winnie could not remember seeing since she was a schoolgirl. Winnie looked at Paul and Janine, their heads still close together. Paul whispered something to Janine. "We are here, Janine," Moira announced their arrival. Janine got up, turned, and asked the children, "Did you enjoy the art exhibition, my darlings?" The children answered together, "Yes, Mummy J." The elder girl asked, "Mummy J, I would love to have extra art lessons. Mummy M says I should ask you again." "The answer is yes, my darling. This is my colleague's wife, Mrs Hunter. She is an art teacher and fully agrees that you should have the opportunity of extra lessons at your school." "Oh, thank you

Mummy J, and Mrs Hunter. I love drawing and painting."
Winnie concluded that the elder girl was Janine's daughter,
Natasha. Obviously, she did not differentiate between Janine
and Moira; they were both 'mummy' to her. Introductions by
Janine followed, "Winnie, Paul, this is Moira and our husband,
Marcus." Paul had stood up and Marcus and Paul shook hands.
Marcus said, "Good to meet you, Paul, and you too, Winnie.
Janine has mentioned you to myself and Moira, Paul."

Again, Janine only mentioning her the previous evening
made Winnie feel as though Paul was living a life she was not
a part of. Janine said to the children, "I think, my darlings,
you should have a table for lunch in the café. The vacant table
near this one is too near the road. Do you agree, Mummy M?"
"I agree, Mummy J, and I'm sure Daddy does too." Janine
said, "Come along, there is a vacant table inside now. We will
go and order your lunch."

The five children dutifully followed Janine into the café.
Moira asked, "Paul, where are the facilities? I know you and
Janine have dined here previously." Paul got up, "At the back
of the café, Moira, upstairs. I will come with you and show
you the way. The stairs are rather steep and narrow." Moira
linked her arm in Paul's, and with the aid of her crutch,
walked with Paul into the café. Marcus sat down and smiled.
"I think you and I, Winnie, can now have a chat about my
Janine and your Paul. Where to start? Two months last
Wednesday, I attended a meeting of senior bank officials here
in the city. It finished at lunchtime and I walked from the
Plaza hotel, intending to have lunch here. Janine had said it
was very good. I reached the bus stop back there and saw, as
you did yesterday, Paul and my Janine coming out of the café.
They were very close to each other. They looked more than

simply colleagues who had lunched. I thought that my lovely wife was involved with another man. Your husband Paul had been mentioned to me with regard to work. As I'm sure you know, he intends to retire in two years' time. I said nothing to Janine about what I had seen. I did, though, talk to Moira. My dear wife knew more than me about the situation, of course. Janine and Moira have confided in each other since they were schoolgirls. Janine did say other things to me from time to time which added to what Moira had told me." Marcus smiled, "To be candid, Winnie, pillow talk between myself and my wives is on a week-by-week basis. This morning I was told about Paul's text when Janine checked her phone, as she always does before we get up. To sum up the situation that exists between my wife and your husband, I will say two things. First of all, both of them are under pressure from a professional point of view, and yes, they complement each other in that respect. Additionally, my Janine feels there is an onus on her to continue to earn a good income as a result of Moira's accident. To be candid, it's not really necessary. Our youngest daughter, Moira's, was just one year old at the time of Moira's accident. Moira's professional life was obviously put on hold. It has taken time for my lovely wife to regain her mobility. A wheelchair is not often needed now. The stair lift will be in use for some time. Moira is going to commence work again on a part-time basis. We have bought a car that is being specially adapted for her. We did hope, prior to Moira's accident, that Janine would become pregnant and give us another little girl to add to our family. This may happen now. Both Janine and Moira give as much time as they can to our children. However, childcare is not a problem, as we employ a nanny. I also spend as much time as I can with our children, although my commitments at the old lady on Thread-needle Street do mean I'm late home some evenings. So Janine feels pressure, and yes, I know that Paul does too. As a senior partner, he is under considerable strain.

At what she had heard, Winnie seethed inside, but she did not let it show. She was not included in Paul's thoughts and plans; retire early? He had told her last night! Janine was the one he talked to, not her. Marcus and Moira knew more about Paul's situation and plans than she did. Again, she felt like an outsider when it came to Paul. Marcus continued, "Yes, two things. I scanned a supplement in a magazine at my club that summed up the situation between my wife and your Paul." Is Paul mine, or is he Janine's? A question in Winnie's head. Marcus continued, "Due to what Janine and Paul are experiencing, the article said they have come together and are having what it termed as an emotional affair. They have bonded more than colleagues generally do." Further comments from Marcus showed he was obviously at ease with the situation in his own mind. "An emotional affair is characterised by non-sexual intimacy. Intimacy shows itself when they are together, sharing an emotional wavelength so to speak. Please hear me out, Winnie, we only have a short time to chat." Winnie thought, some chat indeed. She was the one left in the dark with nothing to say.

As Marcus talked, Winnie observed him and weighed him up. He appeared confident and self-assured, and his public school background evident in his voice, just like Janine and Moira. This background seemed to give him an outer image designed to impress others, As Winnie knew. She could adopt a more upscale manner of speaking if she wished, moving towards what she thought of as a 'higher class' accent and projection of herself. She could assume a public school veneer. In her everyday speech, traces of the local dialect she had acquired during her primary school years were still present. Winnie could also sense that Marcus did not necessarily need to rely on the imagery of his public school background. He seemed to be naturally elevated above others with similar backgrounds. However, the word 'patronised' came to Winnie's mind as she listened to him. She could not help but think of another man who had excelled compared to others in terms of career progression, despite not having a public school background—her dad. Marcus continued, "I do appreciate that I am sharing this with you while being married to two women. Not in the legal sense, but in every other way, they are wives to me, and I'm a husband to both Janine and Moira. There are people who envy me, others are neutral, and some have voiced their objections to our unconventional domestic situation. A former cabinet minister once bluntly told me that I should have married one woman and kept the other as a mistress." Marcus smiled, "It was his preferred arrangement." Winnie couldn't help but think that Marcus was quite open about his situation and seemed pleased and satisfied with his life. Janine, Paul, and Moira returned to the table, and the conversation turned to the menu and ordering meals.

Winnie put her knife and fork down; she could eat no more. The others continued eating. Paul and Janine looked as though they were in a world of their own. Marcus and Moira seemed to be, at face value, unaware of this. To Winnie, the whole point of being there, to be reassured that nothing untoward was taking place between Paul and Janine, meant nothing. It was having the opposite effect. Paul could have sat next to her; no, he had sat next to Janine. It crossed Winnie's mind that she was probably being a little oversensitive. But no, she told herself, stop trying to justify it. Paul obviously preferred Janine's company to hers here and now. Words passed between Paul and Janine; Janine shook her head and Paul nodded. Both of them were smiling. It seemed as though they had a language of their own. She had not been included in their conversation, more excluded. Winnie had reached a point again when she was about to get up and walk away. A voice intervened, "Mummy M and Daddy, must I eat the salad as well as my chicken and fries?" The younger daughter stood next to Janine. Marcus answered her, "Darling, you know Mummy M and Mummy J will expect you to make a tidy plate." Janine got up. "Come along, dear, and show me how you can eat your nice side salad with your chicken and fries together, not on its own." "Yes, Mummy J." Janine and the little girl walked back into the café. Moira watched them smiling. "I'm sure you can appreciate, Winnie, that Lavinia seeks particularly my attention a little more over small things. I have not been there for her, or our other children as much as I would have wished. Janine could not have done more for them than she has." Winnie replied politely, "Yes, Moira, I know from what Paul said it has been a difficult time for you all. We only have one daughter, but 'mummy' is the one children turn to first. Paul and Marcus may not agree." At last, Paul seemed to remember that she was there and said, "No argument from me, Winnie. Our Lorraine always turns to you first. Even now at twenty-five and expecting our grandson, or, as you say, our granddaughter." Winnie felt a little more reassured by what Paul had said. However, the way he turned again to Janine and smiled at her, relaxed was not a word that applied. Janine had returned and sat down.

44

Meals were finished, and a decision was made to skip dessert and have coffee instead. Marcus explained, "We promised our children we would take them to the Odeon to see a Disney film showing there, the one with Mickey Mouse as the sorcerer's apprentice. We need to be there in the next twenty minutes or so." All Winnie wanted was to leave; she could not wait for this situation to be over and done with. Janine, who was the last to finish her meal, got up, "I will skip coffee and check if our children are finished eating and, if all is well, that they have tidy plates. I will promise them ice cream at the cinema. Excuse me, Paul and Winnie." Coffee was served, and then Marcus got up, picking up his cup of coffee. He said, "I will join Janine and see if she needs any help." He smiled, "I will also make sure our children use the facilities upstairs and wash their hands." Paul also stood up, "Excuse me, be back soon."

Moira offered Winnie a cigarette. Winnie took out her 70p lighter from her bag and offered Moira a light. "I'm sure, Winnie, both Janine and Marcus have talked to you about Paul and Janine's close relationship. All I can say is that Janine's state of mind is very much influenced by my situation over the last four years or so. Professional pressure has brought Paul and Janine's closer together. They have become mutually dependent on each other. I realise that Marcus and I have probably been much more aware of this than you have." That comment did not improve Winnie's thoughts about the situation. Moira continued in a superior tone of voice, "From what Janine told me about Paul's text and finding out about Paul and Janine only yesterday, it must have come as a shock." Winnie paused for a moment before she replied, maintaining politeness, "Paul has never mentioned Janine. But you are correct, to find my husband so involved with someone else was indeed a shock." Silenced followed for a few minutes.

Paul returned, followed by Marcus, Janine, and the children. "Now, have we all been upstairs and washed our hands?" The children said in unison, "Yes, Mummy M." Marcus looked at his watch, "I think it's time we made our way to the cinema. Say goodbye to Mr and Mrs Hunter." They said, "Bye-bye, Mr and Mrs Hunter, nice to have met you." Natasha, Janine's daughter, added, "Thank you, Mrs Hunter, for talking to Mummy J about my extra art lessons." What else could Winnie say other than, "I did not mind at all. I hope you enjoy them." Marcus offered his arm to Moira, and with the aid of her crutch, she stood up. Winnie also stood up and put on her new duffel coat. It was easier to wear it than carry it. Moira smiled and said, "I do like your duffel coat, Winnie. I read somewhere that they are back in fashion. Yours has obviously seen some service." "My dad was in the Navy, Moira. He joined at the age of 17, a regular. He served for thirty years." Winnie chose not to add anything further, letting Moira mull over the details. "His preference to working in a factory, like my grandad and my uncle. I grew up in a navy quarter, a house near the base where my dad served and sailed from." "Oh, I see," Moira replied. Her tone of voice telling Winnie what she was thinking. It was a moment of quiet satisfaction for Winnie, and she did not explain any further. Her father had retired with the rank of Rear Admiral, termed by the Navy as lower half. Marcus then said, It was nice to have met you, Winnie, and of course you, Paul." Marcus and Paul shook hands, and Marcus added, "I have taken care of the bill, Paul." "Oh, thanks for that, Marcus. Very nice of you." Paul responded. Janine and Moira also said their goodbyes to

Winnie and Paul. Janine added, "See you on Monday, Paul, bright and early." The children walked ahead of their parents. Janine and Moira walked on either side of Marcus, with Moira needing the aid of her crutch.

Paul smiled at Winnie as though everything was absolutely fine to him. "I will flag down a taxi, Winnie." Paul stepped forward to the edge of the pavement and held out his arm. He was lucky; a taxi pulled over from the other side of the road to the curb. Paul opened the passenger door, and Winnie got in, Paul following her, saying to the driver, "Castle Street station." As the taxi pulled out into the traffic, Paul started to talk. "There you are, Winnie. You now know everything is all right, nothing for you to worry about." Winnie did not reply. Paul carried on talking, "When we get back, there will still be time to call at the hardware shop. Pick up paint, sandpaper, and brushes. I think a large container of white emulsion will be useful. Lorraine's lounge and the bedrooms need a base coat prior to further decoration." Paul then moved on to how he could help Michael, Lorraine's husband, over the coming weekends to make sure their house is nearly decorated throughout as possible prior to their grandchild being born. He continued in this vein the entire journey in the taxi, mentioning that Winnie had designed a garden layout, suggesting she could do the same for Lorraine and Michael. Winnie said nothing, she was full of her own thoughts about the time she had spent in the company of Paul, Janine, and, of course, Moira and Marcus. Paul did not seem to notice. When the taxi stopped at the station, Winnie got out and walked up the slope to the station entrance. Paul followed behind after he had paid the taxi fare.

Paul and Winnie descended the steps to platform two and walked along the platform. Paul was still talking about Lorraine and the house. "So, what do you think about tomorrow, Winnie?" That was it. Winnie's restraint, keeping her thoughts and feelings to herself since Paul had introduced her to Janine, gave way. "Paul, at this moment in time, I couldn't care less. According to you, today was meant to reassure me that you are still my loving husband and not involved with Janine. I feel as though I have lost you. An emotional relationship of a non-sexual nature, Marcus told me, and he and Moira seem quite content with this. To me, you are still cheating in the way you react to Janine. I felt at times as though I need not be there. If you had told me last night that you were taking Janine to bed, I could have more easily dealt with that. As far as I am concerned, you and Janine are mentally shagging each other in your heads. Comments by Moira and Marcus about you and Janine sharing your problems, your fears, and your worries. They may have stood back and rationalised the situation, but that's not for me. You couldn't come to me and talk at all you bared your soul to Janine. As far as I'm concerned, what's the word? Yes, you have betrayed me. I can't go on day-to-day with this in the background. Mary told me she is preparing a room to rent. I will phone her when we get back and ask if I can move in. In my folder back at the house, there are application forms for a full-time post at Grove Academy. I had no intention of filling them in, but now I will. I'm near certain I will get the job. I will teach full-time and be independent of you and away from you for a while. Let's say for two years. On Monday, you can tell this to Janine, and she will no doubt sympathise and comfort you. Oh, and inform her so that Marcus and Moira will find out—like the three of them—I did attend a public school and can turn on a superior middle-class approach if I wish, as you well know. Particularly for Moira, let Janine know my father retired as a Rear Admiral and was knighted for his services. Also, my mum was an associate professor at a university when Mum and Dad married. You could also add that I was commissioned in the Navy Reserve and acted the part of a senior officer's daughter. No doubt, all of this will be passed between them when Janine and Moira take their turn for pillow talk with Marcus. You said I am what I am, and yes, they are what they are. The three of them are very nice to a point, but also more than a little condescending at times. When they looked at me, I think it begged the question for them: how and why did you come to marry me?" Winnie walked away from Paul, walking further down the platform.

A train arrived, slowed, and came to a stop. Doors opened, and people got out as Winnie stepped into a carriage, not the first class. The seats were arranged in pairs with a table in between on the left side of the carriage. Winnie walked down the aisle. An old lady sat in a seat, her head on one side, eyes closed, and her mouth open, asleep. Winnie sat down opposite her. The lady stirred a little and slept on. Winnie heard movement behind her, Paul sitting down? The train moved out of the station. Winnie's mind was in a whirl, flooded with emotions. Married to Paul all these years, and he talks to her, not me. Why? It hurt. No sex involved, I have been told four times, but the intimacy so evident between the two of them. What's the word? Yes, soulmates. If Janine is Paul's soulmate, where does that leave me? Be reassured, Paul said. I might as well not have been there. At times, as far as Paul was concerned, I did not exist. Moira and Marcus seem able just to stand back, having put the situation between Paul and Janine into some sort of perspective. Can I bring myself to do that? Can I? Think, Winnie, think, try and look at this in other ways, Winnie said to herself. Yes, last weekend, as good as always. Paul said last night and this morning he still loves me. He's never brought the office home; is that why he turned to Janine, just as she turned to him with her thoughts of her commitments to her family situation? Moira and Janine have been friends since childhood. Moira's accident would have had as big an emotional impact on Janine as it did on Marcus. Also, five children, one of their mummies injured and disabled, all of them upset. Put on one side what seemed to come across as an assessment of me by their parents. Do I really want to rent a room from Mary and teach full-time? What would Lorraine think of that? I can't do it to her, the baby. Do I really want to give up my home, my studio, and Paul? Think, Winnie, think. I love Paul. Am I being unfair to him? I could support him by working full-time and allowing him to retire before his pension due date. Janine, at some point, could become pregnant and leave before Paul retires. Was it Moira or Marcus who said that's what they had planned, hoped for, prior to Moira's accident? I could contact the art dealer, and all being well, he will buy some of my paintings. Another way of bringing in money for the next two years. Her thoughts were a merry-go-round in Winnie's head. Make a decision, she said to herself, be your father's daughter.

The train was passing between high walls on either side of the track. It would soon reach Braden Street station where Paul and Winnie would get out. Winnie looked to her left. By the side of the line, workmen in high viz jackets and safety helmets were visible, indicating weekend engineering work.

Through the gap between the windows and the seats that she and Paul were sitting on, she could see Paul's reflection in the window. He sat slumped forward, his head in his hands. The train slowed down as the platform came into view. Winnie got up from her seat, turned to her right, and walked two paces forward. She then turned to her right again, facing Paul. Winnie and Paul looked at each other.

Life

The Here and Now

Morris sat down at the kitchen table, relishing a bit of luxury on Good Friday, and enjoying a day off work. It was time to fry bacon and make a sandwich—not just settle for cornflakes for breakfast this Friday morning. After savouring his sandwich—*lovely*, he thought—he buttered a slice of toast and generously spread marmalade on it. Luxury once again! As he carefully put the top back on the marmalade jar, Morris heard the front door swing open. He knew exactly who it was; only one other person had a key to the house: his sister, Emily. "Come in, sis. Sit down. There's a half slice of toast and marmalade waiting for you. Oh, and get a plate and a mug. There's enough tea for the both of us." Emily sat down and responded, "Thanks. I only managed a mug of tea before heading out. The supermarket rang, they were short-staffed. Six hours for me. A late bus got me into town early. With time to spare, I thought I would pop in to see you. Henry is off work today, so he will look after the boys." Morris poured the rest of the tea from the pot into two mugs. "Half and half, sis, just about." Emily looked at him. "Morris, you won't like me saying this, but I have been thinking about talking to you for some time now. You have got to think about how you are living your life. You are drifting. You are still in the house we both grew up in. The front and back gardens are a mess. You looked after them when Mum was alive—flowers, vegetables, and tomatoes from the greenhouse. The house needs decorating inside and out. As for the furniture, it's what Mum and Dad bought in 1939. It's well past its best. Why don't you do the house up, sell it, and find something smaller, more suitable?" Minutes passed away as Morris and Emily ate their toast, Lost in thought.

Morris sighed and picked up a packet of cigarettes from the kitchen table, offering one to his sister. They both lit up, and as Morris exhaled a puff of smoke, he said, "Sis, you might not like what I am going to say. You only want me to sell the house so you can get your hands on half of the bloody cash." Emily started to get up, saying, "I will go now." "No, no wait, me and my big mouth, sorry. Emily, you have got a point, and I can't deny it. I will go, Morris." "No, sit down, please. Look out of the kitchen window, it's pouring down. I'll phone for a taxi. We can wait in the lounge and look out of the window until it arrives. I have done it countless times before."

After he phoned for the taxi, Morris joined Emily in the lounge to look out for and wait for the taxi. He got his wallet out of his trouser pocket, took out £40, and handed it to Emily, saying, "Here's the taxi fare." "Morris, that's more than I will need for a taxi!" Emily exclaimed. "Keep it. Buy yourself a meal and a drink at break time. With what's left, buy the lads an Easter egg from me," Morris insisted. "Thanks, Morris. You are helping me again." Emily expressed her gratitude. "The taxi is here, sis." Morris stated, and went to the front door and opened it. Emily followed him. The taxi driver saw

Morris and waved. He had picked Morris up and dropped him off on a number of occasions. Emily walked out of the house, saying, "Thanks!" Morris watched as his sister got into the taxi.

After the taxi left, Morris closed the front door. He walked back into the kitchen, cleared the table, and sat down. He sat for a few minutes, he then got up, made a mug of instant coffee, and retrieved his packet of cigarettes and lighter from the kitchen table. With his mug of coffee, he went back into the lounge, and stood by the window, gazing outside. He thought about his conversation with Emily. It had almost ended with her walking out, just like the previous week. He had rounded on her then when she had said something he did not want to hear. He must do better. Morris smiled, that had been the written comment on his school reports a number of times.

He looked at the front garden, rain still falling. Yes, Emily was right, a mess. The lawn—he had not mowed it, or the one at the back of the house, for over a year. The rose bushes, their mum had so loved, needed pruning. Morris sat down in a faded armchair, finished his mug of coffee, and put the mug down on the coffee table. One leg of the table supported on a copy of the Oxford Concise Dictionary. The leg broke when he had stumbled into the table one Friday night when he had stupidly joined in a whisky and beer chaser competition with his mates at the club. He had vowed never to drink whisky again!

Morris sat back, lit a cigarette, and looked around the lounge. Lounge? His mum always called it the front room. The lounge had a down-at-heels tired look. He had lived with it for so long he did not notice it. The only new item in the lounge, a large TV. He looked at the fireplace. In the hearth, empty beer bottles and cans: the aftermath of TV evenings.

On the wall above the fireplace was his mother and father's wedding photograph, both of them smiling, his father in uniform—the father he never knew. He had been killed during the last week of the war. Morris had been born two days before a telegram arrived to inform his mum that his and Emily's father was dead. His thoughts went back in time; as he grew up, his mum had been good with him and Emily. His sister was three years older than him. Emily had married, and he continued living with his mum. There was a break when he went to university, returning home for some of the holidays. As the years passed, his mum changed. It reached a point where it seemed all she ever said was a criticism or a complaint. It was a sad memory; he had tried his best, to no avail.

Emily had taken their mum to the GP. She had told the doctor about their Mum's situation. After talking to their mum, he concluded that she was suffering from depression. This was caused by an on-going feelings of grief, which for many years, she had kept hidden, now out in the open. Medication? Useless. Their mum had simply lost the will to live and died three years ago.

Morris stubbed out his cigarette in a nearly overflowing ashtray. He got up from the armchair and walked around the lounge. Dust on the furniture, cobwebs on the lights, faded wallpaper. He sighed and looked at the carpet, noticing crumbs and bits of paper. "I will get the vacuum out," he thought, "I hope the bloody thing still works!" Morris went back into the kitchen and put the kettle on. As he waited for it to boil, he looked around. When was the last time he had moped the kitchen floor? There was a pile of crockery and cutlery he had used in the kitchen sink and on the draining board. He made a mug of instant coffee, sat down at the kitchen table, and lit another cigarette. Emily was right, he was simply drifting, just getting by. And yes, if the house was sold, half of the money would go to Emily, her husband, and his nephews. His thoughts went back. At one point, his future looked bright. A good degree and final examinations to further qualify. His career had been on track. He thought of Sally. He had met Sally during a university holiday in his last year. A year older than him, she had moved to the town to take up articles with a firm of accountants after completing her degree. She had put all the other girls he had taken out, and been with, in the shade. Emily sometimes mentioned Linda, whom he had spent a lot of time with down by the canal during his two years of A-levels studies. He still saw Linda from time to time, still single, at the club. They would chat, and he would buy her drinks, but, she wasn't the one for him. With a touch of sadness, Morris shook his head and said aloud, "Bloody hell, Sally, I really buggered things up with you."

It all blew apart the evening Morris and Sally, now engaged, were at a social event organised by the firm he worked for. He had just come out of the gents, knowing he was slightly tipsy—just a touch 'Brahms and Liszt', As the saying goes. He had vowed to stick to lemonade or coke for the rest of the evening. His memory of what happened next made him exclaim out loud, "fucking hell." Dolly, who was nicknamed 'the bird' by other chaps in the office, exited the ladies' room. Dolly, who back then worked in the next office, had often made it clear that she was quite interested in him. In an instant, Dolly was all over him, saying she loved him. The drink was in and wit was out, he was all over her. Just as he was lost in this encounter, the door to the Lounge Bar opened, and Sally walked in. Morris's tie was askew, shirt buttons undone.

He and Dolly were in each other's arms, and one of Dolly's ample breasts was out of her bra and blouse. Morris recalled what he had said, "Sally, I can explain." He shook his head and said aloud, "Pathetic, no fucking chance." Sally's words came back to him, engraved on his memory: "No explanation needed, Morris. If this is how you carry on when my back is turned." Sally had removed her engagement ring from her finger, turned, and walked back through the door into the Lounge Bar. Dolly still had her arms around his neck, a laugh escaping her lips. Returning to the Lounge Bar, he asked a friend if he had seen Sally. "She left in something of a hurry, mate." The reply came. Phone calls to the office of the firm where Sally worked yielded the same response: "Ms Burton is not available." A visit to the guest house where Sally had a room resulted in the man who ran the guest house, along with his wife, told him, "She says she does not want to be arsed with you, mate. So, sod off." Morris got up from the kitchen table, realising he had smoked three cigarettes—the evidence of ash and cigarette ends scattered amidst half a mug of cold coffee. He cleaned and washed the mug. It was lunch time. He made himself cheese and tomato sandwiches, finding no ham in the fridge. As he ate his sandwiches, washed down with a glass of canned beer, Emily's words echoed in his mind, "You are drifting." Emily was right, he thought as he ate the last bite of his sandwich and drained his glass of beer. Morris then lit a cigarette and thought about his life.

He had not sat his final professional examinations. He was in the same job in the same office. It paid well, more than he needed to keep him afloat. 'Lifestyle' was a word that over gilded the lily. His life had grown monotonous. Tuesday and Friday evenings were spent at the club with Brad and other mates—beer, snooker, cards, and dominoes. Intellectual chat? That revolved around cricket predictions, speculations about the local team's Saturday performance, and a vital question, would Man U come out on top? If that was the extent of what one needed, it seemed satisfactory. On other evenings, the routine consisted of TV and microwave meals. Similar situation was with Brad, he still lived with his mum. Brad, his old school pal, who left school at 16, and served an apprenticeship as a mechanic. He got married at 18, and divorced by 21. At least, as Brad had said, there were no rug rats to complicate his situation. Despite his circumstances, Brad was a good friend. Their weekends were predictably uniform. Saturday lunchtime was marked by a beer and a pasty at the Kings Arms, followed by an afternoon either in a snooker club or at a local match if the team was playing at home. Evening's featured a choice between a film at the Odeon or the Gaumont, followed by a nightcap or two at the Kings Arms. Sundays were for fishing, with Brad, if the weather was fine. They always packed their fishing kit up just before opening time. On wet days, they would resort to reading books, perusing the Sunday papers, and watching TV. Lunchtime involved meeting Brad at the club for beer, followed by a takeaway from the Dynasty, a Chinese restaurant. Holidays consisting of fishing trips, staying at the same guest house. A cooked breakfast and readily available beer were part of the package. Morris let out a sigh, recognising the unchanging routine—the same old, same old, week after week, year after year. "Oh Sally, Sally, I still miss you," he said to himself. Other girls? Yes, he and Brad had taken girls out from time to time, picking them up at pubs, dances, or while on holiday. Some were very accommodating, as Brad put it. Nice as they might have been, none were the right fit for him or Brad. They had stopped going to dances at the Mecca after Brad commented that the majority of the age group there looked young enough to be still in the Brownies. As for afternoon tea dances at the Trades Hall on Saturdays? "Bugger that for a game of toy soldiers!"

He had seen Sally twice. The first time, Sally was going into a shop with a little girl and a man—her husband and their daughter, he had presumed. It hurt; Sally had married someone else. The second time, Sally was on a bus, sitting with a little boy wearing a school cap. The bus had stopped at a traffic light, and as Morris and Brad walked past, Morris stole a glance at it. Morris sat for a moment or two and then said aloud, "You're right, Emily. I need to change. I need to sort my life out. It starts here and now."

Life Moves On

In the kitchen, Morris put two eggs into a pan of boiling water, buttered bread, and made a pot of tea. After he had eaten and washed up, he looked around the kitchen. The floor was mopped, tile surfaces wiped down. The piled-up crockery and cutlery washed and returned to the cupboard and drawer. The lounge and hall were cleaned of clutter, vacuumed, and dusted. His bedroom had been a challenge. When was the last time he had changed and washed the bed linen? The three spare bedrooms were given a damp dust and vacuuming, which did the trick. The washing machine in the kitchen and the tumble dryer in the garage were working overtime. He glanced into the dining room but quickly closed the door, deciding it could wait!

Morris watched the 6 o'clock news on TV and sat down to read a book afterwards. At eight o'clock, he left the house and walked to the club. As usual for a Friday evening, he knew there would be fish and chips on the way back home. How long would this routine last? He did not want to think about it. Morris walked into the club's saloon bar. Brad who always arrived earlier, was not s in his usual seat with the other four regulars they always sat with. Without delay, Sean told him with a grin, "Brad's taking Linda out for a meal, and they are going out for the day tomorrow. I saw him in the corner shop near my lodging; he asked me to tell you, mate." Morris looked at Sean and said, "Good of him. There are better things in life than being here on a Friday evening. Now, it's my shout, I will get around in. Shall we play cards or dominoes, or shall we sort out Man U's and Liverpool's chances first?"

On Saturday, Morris phoned two decorating firms and arranged to get quotes on Tuesday and Wednesday evenings. Both inside and outside of the house to be quoted for. Money was not a problem; he rarely spent more than half of his salary. He also contacted a gardening service business, scheduling a quote for Tuesday evening. Morris drove into the town and parked in his designated spot at the Mason and Lawson Architects' car park—the firm he worked for. His was the only car parked there. Two hours later, he walked out of Gorton & Sons tailors with carrier bags. Two new suits to replace the ones he was currently working in. Additionally, he had purchased a jacket and two pairs of trousers. He had a new jacket on, shirt, and trousers. The clothes he had been wearing when he went into the tailors now disposed of in a bin. The shoes, shirts, and ties he had bought from shops near the firm's car park were in the boot of his car. Morris was content with his purchases; his down at heels look outside office hours would soon be a thing of the past. Now, he thought, he should take the carrier bags to his car's boot and then enjoy some lunch. Morris whistled as he walked down the high street.

As he walked past the window of Barnet and Son estate agents, he stopped. He looked into the window at properties for sale. Morris new the senior salesman; he had dealt with him from a business point of view. He could see Mark Langford talking to a member of staff. The house—get on with it, he thought—a ballpark value as a start. Morris opened the door and went in. "Morris, hello, how are you?" Mark greeted. "Fine, thanks, Mark. I think I can put a little business your way." "No problem, Morris. I owe you a couple of favours." Morris and Mark sat down in Mark's office. After five minutes of conversation, Mark surprised Morris. "To sum up, Morris, your house—detached, gardens, four bedrooms, dining room, lounge, and kitchen—being the classic ten minutes' walk to the station, will easily fetch half a million plus. As I'm sure you know, people in London are selling up, moving here, and commuting. What they sell for, your house will be a steal for them. Decorate it to spruce it up and tidy the gardens. Leave the kitchen; if you put a new one in, a buyer will probably strip it out and start again. I could come and give you a valuation on Monday. Yes, bank holiday Monday—you will be on holiday, but this office is open."

Mark laughed. "In this business, we are always bloody well open. My wife says she can't work out how we ended up with four children! Now, I will go and get you some property details and organise a coffee." Mark was as good as his word and left Morris in his office with a coffee and a number of property details.

After ten minutes, Mark returned. Morris offered him a cigarette. Mark sat down and exhaled smoke. "You have had a look at those, now here is one at a price that comes along from time to time." Mark gave Morris details of a property in the village of Thorpe Mullen. Morris knew it well; he had driven through it numerous times on his way to the riverside spot where he and Brad preferred to fish. The pub in the village was also very familiar to him. The property details were concise: a cottage with three bedrooms, lounge, dining room, kitchen, and gardens. The detail that caught his eye was the rear garden with a boat jetty on the river, complete with fishing rights. Morris looked at the price; it had been reduced twice. "This looks good, Mark. And it's only twenty to thirty-minute commute to the office." "Yes, Morris, it's a good option. Essentially, it's the kind of property people look at, like, and enthuse about, but they often don't come back. The vendor, he and his family, are currently living in temporary accommodation in Cambridge. They must sell this property in order to be able to buy there due to a job relocation. They spent a fortune on the place doing it up. He was on the phone this morning, and the bottom line is now £300,000, no less. It's a bargain." Morris sat back and thought for a moment. "Mark, between you and I, I could run to that and be back in the money when my house sells." Mark said, "Okay, I did say I owed you a favour. We actually live in the village, in the house opposite the pub. I will take the keys with me, and if you wish, you can view the place tomorrow, say about four thirty?" "I will be there, Mark. Thanks." "No problem. I will be asking you for a favour next week. It's in my desk diary to phone you. It's about a conversion job—the old Mill on Lower Street, more apartments. Now, client due, one property I will not tell him about! See you tomorrow."

Morris walked down the high street, feeling content. Yes, life was about to change. Not only for him, but also for Emily. What she and her husband, Henry, would get after the sale of the house would make a big difference to them and his nephews, Terry and Adam. He smiled to himself. He had taken the boys fishing from time to time. Now, if everything worked out with the cottage, they could enjoy fishing with him from the back garden. He thought about the house where Mark and his family lived. Opposite the pub, behind high walls with a security gate. Morris and Brad had often parked at the pub after a day of fishing.

He had worked with Mark a number of times on several occasions for commercial property developments. There had been commissions for him, and as Mark had said, there were more opportunities to come. His only thought, right now, was to get his carrier bags in the car's boot and have something to eat. Morris looked at his watch, it was already 2 p.m.— lunchtime. And then, it happened—the major change in his life.

In the near distance, and man, a lady, and two children stood outside McWhities burger bar. As Morris drew nearer, he knew who the lady was—it was Sally. Other people passing by looked at Sally and the man, and the two children stood to one side, their arms wrapped around each other. Sally was being talked at, a wagging finger accompanying the scolding. Morris was now near enough to hear what was being said, and he stopped. Neither the man nor Sally noticed him. The finger waged on. The man said, "If you think you are getting any money out of me for those two, you can bloody well think again. I'm out of a job, on benefits, and I'm going to stay that way until the divorce is finalised. Not a fucking penny is coming your way." Sally asked, "Richard, please give me enough money now to buy them something to eat. You are their father." "No way. If you want money, you can leave them at the burger bar and do whatever with some guy, for all I fucking care. It was all up with you when I caught you reading those letters from that posh bloke at university—the one you told me about. And you had the ring he gave you on your finger. Giving you another slap or two will make my fucking day." As Sally's soon-to-be ex-husband stepped forward with his arm raised, Morris swiftly put his carrier bags down and stepped between them. He faced Richard, and while Morris enjoyed a beer or two himself, the man's breath was potent enough to stop a bus. "I'm the one, dickhead, who sent those letters and bought Sally the engagement ring. If you're looking for a fight, you will have to go through me first. So, take a swing. It's been a few years since I boxed back at university, but a right or left cross from me will put a weedy-looking like you on the pavement." "The man," Richard, backed away. He then turned and walked away, looking back twice to swear at Morris. Morris turned to face Sally, smiled and said, "Hello, Sally. Remember me? I arrived just in time to hear you are getting a divorce." Morris glanced down at the girl and the boy, who have moved closer to their mum. "Yes, Morris, you overheard what he said about your letters and the ring you gave me. I read your letters again and again when I was on my own. I never forgot you, Morris. I'm not much now compared to when we were together. I married him on the rebound after, well, we both remember why I walked out on you. It all went downhill from the start. I couldn't get away from him. I was two months pregnant the day I married him. You might as well know that. The only silver lining for me is my daughter and son. Joan is nine, and Andrew is seven. Morris, I will say no more—you probably have someone to go home to. I will let you go." Morris looked at Sally, Joan, and Andrew. All three of them were dressed in well-worn clothing; evidently, very little money had been spent on clothes. "No, Sally, I'm not going to leave. There's no one waiting for me. All I have to go back to is an empty house. The three of you need a meal and a place to sit down." Morris looked at Joan and Andrew and said, "Now, the two of you, if you eat all your vegetables, there's ice cream to follow, and coke to drink. What do you say?" There were smiles and cries of, "Yes, please." "Come on then, it's not far. I will put my carrier bags in my car, and we will soon be at the restaurant. It's a good place—I eat there Monday to Friday."

Life Changes

After they had eaten, Morris suggested a walk in the park. They walked around the gardens, and Sally's children ran to the playground with its swings, slides, and other amusements. As Joan and Andrew played happily on the swings, Morris and Sally sat on a bench, and watched them. "Where do you live now, Sally?" Morris inquired. "We are in a one-bedroom flat. All the council had to offer was a bedsit. The rent is expensive; it takes over half of the benefits I receive. That's why I asked him to help me. He has never been much of a father. I was always short of money; beer and gambling came first. He wouldn't let me work part-time during school hours. All three of us were frightened of him. Sorry, Morris, I will say no more." They sat in silence for a minute or so. "Sally, I still live in the same house; remember, you visited when my mum was still alive. It's going to be spruced up and sold. There are three spare bedrooms, yes, one for you Miss Burton." Sally smiled at the mention of her family name. Morris continued, "Rent-free, of course, and I will buy groceries on the way there. What do you think, Sally?"

"Thanks, Morris, that will be lovely. It will give me a chance to sort things out. I've got to organise a stable future for Joan and Andrew. Get a part-time job to bring money in and get away from being too dependent on benefits. The school? How can I get them there? I don't want them to have to change; they are happy at their present school." "Slow down, Sally. A week's holiday before school starts again. You could drive—I remember. Next week you can try my car. A VW Golf is a lovely car to drive. Easter Monday will be a good day for you to try it out; there will not be much traffic in town."

"Thanks again, Morris. How would you get to work?"
"No problem, we work on a flexi basis. I have spent many hours at work rather than go home to an empty house. I can catch a bus or take some time off. I have days owing to me."

A moment or two passed, Joan and Andrew still happily playing on the swings. "Sally, tomorrow I am going to view a cottage. Would you like to come with me? It's in the village of Thorpe Mallon. There's a pub there, the Crown, they serve meals and it's very nice inside." "That would be nice, Morris, a treat. But no thank you, you have treated us already. I can't let you do it again." "Oh yes, you can, Sally, my phone's back at the house; it needed charging. There's a phone box by the Park gate. I will be back in five minutes or so."

Morris sat down on the bench, "Table booked for one-thirty, Sally. We will get to the Crown for one, time for a drink." "Thank you, Morris, thank you." Joan and Andrew were now playing on a roundabout, Joan had one foot on the ground from time to time to keep it moving. "They're happy now, Sally, and things should be better for them now they are free of him." "All I can say for myself, Morris, is that I tried my best to make it work for my children."

Again a moment or two passed. Morris glanced at Sally, smiling as she watched Joan and Andrew. "Sally, have you still got the ring I gave you?" "Yes, I still have it. He tried to take it from me, saying he would sell it. I ran out of the house and hid it in the garden and told him I had thrown it away. I will say nothing about what happened next. Your ring is in a zip pocket in my shoulder bag." "Can I see it?" Sally looked at Morris and then opened her bag, taking out the ring with three rubies. She gave it to Morris, who looked at it and said, "Sally, I think what I am going to say will sound like something from fiction. Over the years since we parted, there have been others, but none of them could replace you. I can't even remember their names. I never got over you, Sally, I still love you. Please give me your left hand." Sally did as he asked. Morris put the ruby ring on the ring finger of Sally's left hand. "Sally, I will ask you again, will you marry me?" Sally looked at him, smiled, tears in her eyes. "Oh yes, Morris. I thought of you often and, as I said, I read your letters to me many times." They embraced each other, sharing a kiss. A wolf whistle from Andrew, and shouts of, "Mummy, Mummy!" from Joan. Morris turned his head, his arms still around Sally. He smiled and called out, "Now, how about the four of us go out on the park lake in a rowing boat, and afterwards, drinks, cakes, and more ice cream in the park café?" Shouts off, "Yes, please, bring it on!" came from Andrew, and "Lovely, yes, please!" from Joan.

"Morris, you will get them overexcited." "No problem. I don't think there's been much for them to be excited about in the past. Afterwards, we will go to the place you have been living in, get your clothes and other belongings, buy groceries, and go to my house to get the three of you settled in. Oh, another thing, my future wife and my future stepchildren are going on a shopping trip next week. New clothes, shoes, and anything else they need."

Life as Lived

The day was warm, the sun shone, not a cloud in the sky. A cool breeze from the sea rustled through the palm trees. Waves broke gently on the sand. Morris sat up, watching as Joan and Andrew threw a ball to each other playing happily in the sea. Both of them could swim better than he could.

Morris waved, and they waved back. It had taken time for them to get used to him, and for him to get used to them. Now they both called him dad. Morris looked at Sally lying beside him in her bikini. Sunglasses shaded her eyes, a smile on her lips. Next to Sally, in her carry-cot with a sunshade, their daughter Angela cooed and made happy noises. Angela had just turned one year old two days ago. Morris lay back again, happy and content. From the moment Sally came back to him, his life had been worth living again.

Only on TV

Tamara sat down in the lounge with a plate of buttered toast and a cup of tea. *I will have to go to the shops*, she thought, *there's nothing much left to eat in the house. There's only some meat in the freezer and vegetables in the garden.* Tamara had not cooked since last Thursday; she had no interest in cooking or eating food. She had been surviving only on snacks since he left. After finishing her toast and tea, she let out a sigh. It was Thursday again, marking a week since he left. Her thoughts went back prior to last Thursday. Life had seemed normal then. She had been very happy with him and believed he was happy with her as well. On last Saturday night, they had been together as husband and wife, feeling united and inseparable.

However, hints of what was to come had been there. On Sunday, he played golf as he often did, and when he returned home later, he had told her that he had started discussing politics with his friends at the 19th hole. Monday evening passed by pleasantly. They had watched a repeat episode of Morse, one they had not seen before. After the show, their conversation veered towards relationships. She had said, "The man who was betrayed because his wife was having an affair, suspected of killing her and later cleared, he had someone in

70

the background who loved him and wanted to be with him."
He had then remarked, "It was the same in the repeat of Vera,
but the other way around: the woman suspected and cleared,
with a man in the background who was in love with her."
They had previously watched an episode of Vera. "Part of the
drama to provide a happy ending," he added. "It could only
happen on TV," echoing her own words. What he had said
next stung now, "There can't be that many people having
affairs in real life; as you say, it's mostly on TV. Often, an
affair is a requirement of the plot."

Tuesday evening passed as normal; with nothing
untoward. They had enjoyed a lovely time in bed together
again, and even had a discussion about starting a family
during a pillow talk. How could he have talked about that with
her when he knew what he was planning? On Wednesday
evening, bringing another hint of what was to come. On
Wednesday evenings, he had a routine of meeting up with his
old school friends at the local pub, the Crown and Anchor.
They would enjoy beer, play darts, and chat. In the past, he
used to leave the house at nine in the evening. However, for
the past few weeks, he had been leaving as early as seven.

Up to last Thursday, her working week had been as
normal. The end of term meant more play activities from a
learning point of view, which was the usual approach in
primary schools during the last week of term prior to the
summer holiday. Her day at school finished at 3:30, and as
usual, she would be home by four. There was plenty of time,
as always, to prepare their evening meal. New potatoes were
dug up from the garden, and pea pods were collected from the
row. He was always home at six, and everything had been
ready.

He entered the kitchen, and she greeted him with a smile, moving towards him for a kiss while saying, "I've prepared your favourite meal." However, he stepped away from her, and said, "This is for you." He held out an envelope, and she automatically took it from him. He then said, "I will not be dining with you. The envelope contains divorce papers. I have met someone else whom I would rather be with." His words stung deeply. He continued, "I will split all savings equally with you. You can stay in the house for a couple of months while you find somewhere else to live. The house will have to be sold, and half of the money it sells for will be yours. You can take any of the furniture you wish. After that, I will have no commitment to you. You are independent of me with your teaching salary. I have all the clothes and personal possessions I wish to take. Whatever else is left in the house, you can dispose of." Those were the last words he said to her before turning and walking out of the kitchen, leaving the house.

Yes, it still hurt. However, gone now, the floods of tears and the feeling of somehow being detached from the situation, as though it must be happening to another woman, not her. The question was still in her mind: how could her marriage and life with him have ended like this? He had not said sorry or goodbye. His approach had seemed to convey, or imply, that the four years they had been together, married for three, was for him simply water under the bridge. The last meal she had cooked for them—lamb cutlets, new potatoes, and garden peas—thrown in the kitchen bin. Gravy and the dish of freshly prepared mint sauce washed away down the kitchen sink.

On the Friday morning, she had phoned the school to say she was unwell—the first time she had missed the last day of term. The day had been spent in tears, her mind in a turmoil.

72

The question she had kept asking herself was where had she been lacking as a wife? For her, he had been the love of her life. She now knew she was not the one to blame. She glanced at the sideboard—next to their wedding photograph was a vase with flowers in it. Last Saturday morning, the doorbell had rung. She had not answered it. From behind a curtain in the lounge, she had looked to see who was there. Roger, the deputy head, walked back down the garden path, got into his car, and drove away. On the front doorstep were the flowers, now in the vase, and a large box of chocolates. A card said, "From your pupils and their parents, thank you." She thought about Roger, who had been married three years ago. Roger and his wife were on their honeymoon, walking down a street in a far eastern country he had never named. Two youths on a motor scooter had snatched his wife's shoulder bag. She was pulled along and hit her head on the road. Dianna, her name, had died eight hours later in a hospital bed. Roger often chatted to her when they were on playground duty, and at other times. It had taken months for him to get over his wife's death. Roger was a very nice, considerate, attentive, and courteous with her. He was also very good with other members of staff. So, she was not alone with an unexpected event in life. Tamara got up from the settee—the least she could do was sort the flowers out. Some blooms were dead, while others still looked quite nice.

The telephone rang. She went into the hall to answer it. "Hello Tamara, it's Roger. I was in Tesco this morning and bumped into you-know-who. He was with another woman, and they were holding hands. He told me you were parting, getting divorced. If you feel like talking to someone, I could call around. Our conversations in the playground and at other times were a great help to me. And I think you know I have always enjoyed being with you. If you wish to talk to me, I could be there in twenty minutes." Tamara paused before she answered, questions in her head. Someone in the background in love with her? Only on TV?

The Viola

The last night at sea. He sighed. What he had planned to say
to his wife of thirty-eight years left unsaid. "Do you enjoy
looking at the moonlight on the sea?" He turned from the
ship's rail, the one person on the ship he would have given his
right arm to talk to and meet during the cruise speaking to him.
"Oh, hello. Yes, the sea is calm tonight and the ship is cruising
so slowly there is very little movement on the water. It helps
me to relax and find peace of mind." She smiled. Even in
artificial light, she was very attractive, and he wanted to move
closer to her. He resisted the temptation. "After fourteen days
on a cruise, you are still looking for peace of mind? We dock
tomorrow at seven in the morning, and your nights at sea will
be over. However, James, enough of that for now. Yes, I know
your name, and I'm certain you know mine." More than a
little surprised she knew his name, he replied, "Yes, yours is
in the brochure, Lumita. I have read the brochure a number of
times, what it says about you, your background, and the others
in the quartet. I think you were going to say something further,
Lumita." She smiled, and the look she gave him said she knew
much more about him than he was aware of. "Yes, James, I
have much more to say to you. I first saw you with your wife
at the concert the quartet gave to welcome passengers on

board the first day of the cruise. You have been to listen to the quartet every time we have played. I have looked for you. Sometimes you were with your friend, or alone. Never after the first time with your wife." James looked at her and replied, "True, she did not wish to join me. To be candid, I was happy about that. However, I have had the impression that there was a reason for this. She normally enjoys classical music, the quartet being a feature of this cruise. I was content when alone; I could not take my eyes off you. That probably makes me sound like an adolescent schoolboy. Also, you play the viola. I can play the violin reasonably well. The viola, I know, is more difficult to play. A larger fingerboard which requires different fingering. The sound, though, so rich and full." "You have a good ear for music, James. Tell me about yourself."

"It's not dramatic stuff, to be candid with you. I got married. I met my wife on the first day of the first week of our first year at university. We married just over three months later. We have a daughter aged nineteen." James smiled, "That tells you why we married. Our daughter is a very independent young lady and is currently backpacking with friends in Europe. Only home for a few days prior to starting her second year at Oxford. So, at thirty-eight, I lecture and teach philosophy at a provincial university. My friend who is on the cruise, with his wife, also works there. His subject is economics. You also studied the dismal science, according to the brochure about the quartet. A first in music and economics at Royal Holloway, London." "You are right, James. I will tell you more about myself. But, first, please tell me more about why you are spending time alone on deck most evenings. I have seen you here but have been unable to speak to you, as I was involved, as the quartet must be, in socialising with first-class passengers." "No problem, Lumita. I come up on deck after dinner for a cigarette, and then some evenings I've joined my wife and our friend's at the show. I will not be missed. My wife will think I have gone to the gentleman's lounge for a cigar. So, back to peace of mind, a chap we knew at university by the name of Greg Sangston reappeared about 10 months ago. At university, I put him in the gutter for sniffing around my wife after we were married. Her being pregnant, not showing at that point in time. I saw her with Greg one lunchtime. Silly really, I bought a magazine at WH Smith and as I left the shop, on the other side of the street, I saw my wife in Greg's arms, kissing before he got into a taxi. I also know bits and pieces about their affair. My wife talks in her sleep. If she is still awake when I go to the cabin, no words will pass between us, not even good night. I was going to confront her with what I knew today, the last day of the cruise. My friend and his wife, being on board and whose company we have been in on a regular basis, stopped that. I had no idea they had booked this cruise. I will have a conversation with my wife during our drive back to the house. Yes, the house I once thought of as home. I will divorce her, sell the house, and move on. It will be messy for a time living under the same roof. I will be damned first before I move out prior to the house selling. Our daughter will have to be told, of course, an upset situation for her but it will have to be done. In preparation for the change in my life, I applied for a post at the LSE. There was an interview and I was successfully appointed. I have already handed my notice in at my present university and will start my work at the LSE at the commencement of the next academic year. All being well, my share of the money from the sale of the house will enable me to make a down payment on something small in London. She, who will be my ex-wife soon, knows nothing of this yet. What happens to her with regard to Greg, I could not care less. I never strayed once, in my working world, although I had many chances. Sorry if I bored you with my problems, but I have at last been able to talk to you, and as the saying goes, get it off my chest."

"Not a problem, James. I can tell you more about Greg and the affair your wife is having with him, but first, I will tell you more about myself. An adolescent boy, you said. When I first saw you, I was a schoolgirl again, with a crush on somebody—you, James. I was born in Romania; my mother died when I was 10. My father's business interests were attracting the attention of the government, so we moved to London overnight. I have British, Irish, and US passports. My father has many contacts and diverse business interests. He is currently enjoying the company of his fourth wife in the presidential suite on deck two. My current stepmother is two years younger than me. I'm thirty-six. She will go eventually with a substantial sum of money which, to my father, will be loose change. He has been a very good father to me. I am financially independent. I do not ask where the money comes from. He assures me that nothing illegal is involved, although I think some of his business deals, shall we say, are in a grey area of activity. I play with the quartet because I enjoy doing so. I have no need of the fees. I was married, and I have a daughter. Anna is twelve years old and is a boarder at my old school, Roedean. I will be picking her up for the holidays in two days' time." "You are divorced, Lumita?" "Yes, but not in a conventional way. My husband worked for my father. He was less nice to me after we married, as previously I knew he

78

was siphoning substantial sums of money from my father's business interests. My father told me that he tolerated this for a time for me and his granddaughter. My husband went too far with a mistress. She also worked for my father and assisted my husband in stealing money. My father is charming, pleasant, and seems easy-going but don't cross him. My husband and his mistress were sent to a warm country by my father where what is in nature should not be taken for granted. They were told by a very friendly local associate of my father that it was safe to swim in a large pool below a waterfall on a river. It was not the best advice. Their identification was found in clothing on the riverbank. I was a widow at the age of thirty-one. You have met my father, James. On the second occasion, he told me you insisted on paying for the Havana cigars and the brandy in the Cigar Lounge. You discussed with him contemporary philosophers Nussbaum, Zizeit, and Badiou. It was a lengthy discussion until two in the morning. My father is very well-read and you impressed him a lot. He told me he enjoyed talking to you and hoped to discuss other writers with you later someday. I thought you should know more than a little about me, my background. It's not, shall we say, conventional."

"I will tell you now, James, what I know about Greg and your wife. Do you wish me to go on?" "Yes, Lumita, please do." "After seeing me play on the first day at lunchtime, your wife avoided being seen again for her own reasons. I was introduced to her by Greg at a social function after the quartet had played there. It was a charity event. She was an old university friend, Greg said. I did see her with Greg again at another function where the quartet played." "What you are telling me, Lumita, fits in with what I know. Overnight trips to London with friends from the office where my wife works to go and see a show. That's what I was told. Tell me more, please." "I will. Greg's soon-to-be ex-wife is an old school and university friend of mine. She plays violin in an orchestra. I know quite a lot about Greg and your wife being together. Greg also has other female interests, where your wife stands with regard to him is an open question."

"Now, regarding the future, yours and mine. As you have said, you will have to inform your wife that you are divorcing her. The main hotel in the city where you currently live is the Manor. My father owns it, one of a chain. I could book a suite there and take my daughter to see the sights—the castle, the Minster, and of course the Roman ruins. You could join us, James. Don't say nothing for the moment. I could also assist you when you come to London to take up your post at the LSE. My apartment is in Knightsbridge, and this could also solve your accommodation problem. No, James, don't say nothing yet, please. You have stood close to me and held my left hand since you mentioned the fingerboard on the viola." "Sorry, Lumita, I should not have done that." "No need to apologise, my dear James. I will now put my arms around your neck, and please put your arms around my waist. Kiss me, James."

"There's a question for you, James. Will the adolescent boy marry the schoolgirl with a crush on you when you are divorced and be a daddy to her daughter?" "Oh yes, Lumita, I will. I have loved you from a distance from the first time I saw you. When the quartet played, I only heard the rich tones of the viola as I looked at you."

James and Lumita held each other close and kissed as the ship increased speed at midnight in order to be in Southampton at seven in the morning.

Golf

Delia walked along a familiar cemetery path with flowers she had bought from the stall at the cemetery gate. She stopped at his grave and read again the inscription. 'In memory. Derek Brownlee. [Year of Birth]—[Year of Death]. Husband of Delia. Rest in Peace'. Her dear Derek had retired early; he only enjoyed 13 months of retirement. It had been three weeks since his funeral. Delia had visited his grave every other day since. The flowers in the grave vase wilted, so she would replace them. On the gravel in the grave surround, there was a wreath with a card attached to it saying simply, 'In Remembrance'. Delia looked at it, thinking it was probably Sybil, Derek's sister, who had placed it there. There had been little contact with Sybil over the years. She and her husband had attended the funeral. There were many other people there, some she recognised, others she did not. Sybil had called last week and promised to keep in touch. Delia did not attend the wake, with nibbles and drinks arranged by the funeral people. All she had wanted to do was go home after her darling husband's funeral.

Delia removed the wilted flowers, finding there was still water in the vase. She carefully arranged the fresh flowers to her satisfaction and stood up. It had been just over six weeks since her dear Derek had passed away. The memory of that day returned vividly. She had prepared lunch and gone to tell him it was ready. He was seated in his armchair, the morning paper he had been reading when she left him, was now on the floor. He did not answer her when she spoke to him, and when she put her hand on his shoulder, he did not move. It was a brain haemorrhage, as the post-mortem revealed. With tears running down her cheeks, Delia walked back down the path towards the cemetery gates. She paused at a point where another path branched off to the right. There lay a small grave near the end of that path, close to a wall. Delia and Derek used to visit it often on Sunday mornings after communion. It was Friday today, and she knew she would visit that grave on Sunday as usual, bringing flowers.

Delia parked her car in the driveway, noticing Derek's car still in the garage. She opened the front door, went in, and closed it behind her. She opened the door of the cloaks cupboard in the hallway intending to hang her fleece up. On the left side of the cupboard were Derek's golf clubs. Delia stood for a moment, reminiscing about Derek's love for golf. He used to play regularly on Saturdays, often staying for drinks and a meal with his friends in the evening. Sometimes he would be away for the whole weekend, participating in charity events at different gold clubs. Delia had never minded his golfing escapades; she knew it brought him joy and relaxation. She believed golf was his way of escaping the worries, problems, and challenges of the business world. As Delia walked down the hallway and into the kitchen, her mind remained occupied with memories of Derek and his love for golf. He had, for many years, with business associates, spent a week at a golf resort in Spain. She had always looked forward to his return, as he was loving and affectionate, brought presents, flowers, and greeted her with a kiss. They had also gone on holidays together, of course, although they never chose places with beaches and children playing. These were cherished memories. As for his golf clubs, clothes, car, and other possessions, she knew she would have to deal with them at some point. Just not yet. At least he had been able to enjoy more time on the golf course during his retirement. Although, one thing puzzled Delia—he had never seemed interested in watching golf on television.

In the kitchen, Delia heard the clock in the hall strike twelve. She decided to prepare something to eat; Mr Lawton, the solicitor, would arrive at one thirty to go through Derek's will. During a phone call, he had mentioned that there were some matters to resolve prior to telling her about Derek's wishes. Mr Lawton also said that he would visit her at home rather than her going to his office—a considerate gesture, Delia thought. Delia got two plates and two soup bowls out of a cupboard, along with a cutlery for two out of a drawer. She stopped as she was about to take a tin of mushroom soup (Derek's favourite) from another cupboard, tears welled up again, thinking Derek was still with her. Just last week, she had thought of something to tell him and had walked into the lounge before remembering he was no longer there. Delia put the crockery and cutlery back in the cupboard and drawer. She would eat later. Delia made herself a cup of coffee, and decided to sit in the lounge and wait for Mr Lawton to arrive.

Delia sat down in the lounge with her coffee. On the coffee table lay an evening newspaper, now four weeks and four days old. It was open at the page containing an obituary for Derek. She picked it up, she had read it often. She read once more about Derek's background, his mum and dad, and where he was born. His education was highlighted—earning a double first from Cambridge in the fields of maths and physics. It also mentioned his postgraduate diploma in Management studies. Delia paused, memories flooding back. Derek had been studying for the diploma part-time when they first met. She read on about his career, culminating in him becoming managing director of Gleston and Sons Manufacturing PLC. The obituary listed his other directorships as well. The year of their marriage was mentioned next, along with her maiden name, Delia Jane Langston, and the fact that she was at that time a successful opera singer. The memories came rushing back—how she and Derek had met in a pub often frequented by casts of the Royal Opera House. The producer had announced at the end of a rehearsal, in his flamboyant style, "Pray join me for a libation at my favourite watering hole!"

Delia had not wanted to go, but she was persuaded to join the gathering. There was a man, on his own, standing at the bar waiting to be served as Delia and other members of the cast entered the bar. He was soon surrounded by them. Delia found herself standing next to him, chatting and laughing with other members of the cast to her right. When she turned to her left, she saw the man was looking at her. She smiled and said, "Looks like we have unintentionally pushed you out of the way, please allow me to make up for it with a drink." Delia and Derek spent the rest of the afternoon and evening together. Derek was in London to attend a two-day conference on behalf of the firm he worked for. On the following two evenings, Derek met Delia after her performances. The performances continued for further three weeks. On subsequent weekends, Derek travelled to London on Saturdays to meet Delia after her performances in Carmen. They spent Sundays together. While Delia fulfilled her contractual obligations, singing in London and then moving on to sing at the Teatro Alla Scala in Milan, they stayed in touch via telephone calls. Delia also made sure to send Derek postcards with heartfelt messages. The cards found their place in an album tucked away in a drawer, not looked at for many years, until recently. Her last commitment was to sing at the Semper Opera House in Germany. Derek travelled to Dresden for the occasion, marking his first and last time sitting among an audience of opera enthusiasts. He watched and listened to his Delia act and sing the part of Violetta in her last performance of La Traviata. When they met afterwards, Derek's first words were a question. He asked Delia to marry him. She had given up her career with its international travel. All she wanted was to be with her lovely Derek. Delia continued reading the obituary, which then mentioned a passing reference to Derek's interest in golf. The last paragraph read that Derek was survived by his wife, Delia, and a sister named Sybil. No other names were listed.

There had been more unforgettable memories. Their first year of marriage could be described, some might say over gilding the lily, as idyllic. Delia only sang arias for her Derek now. He loved listening to her. Derek's career progressed, and they bought the house she would continue to live in. They had both agreed that they needed to have a family to complete their lives together.

Delia looked at the photographs on the sideboard. One of her and Derek in evening dress. She could not remember if it had been taken on their honeymoon on the cruise ship or at a dinner dance. There were other photographs too. Her eyes moved over them until her gaze fell on the last two. The first photograph showed Derek standing in the garden, smiling, with their baby son Keith In his arms. The next one showed Keith asleep in his carrycot. The memory of Keith and Derek together brought tears to her eyes. Two miscarriages and then success—Keith was born. One year, three weeks, and two days later, Keith inexplicably passed away in his sleep. After Keith's death, their lives changed in a way that many would find disconcerting. Derek never mentioned anything about it to Delia. He continued to be a loving, thoughtful, and considerate husband. He encouraged Delia to sing again, on an amateur basis locally, or semi-professionally, and hinted they should try for another child. Suffice it to say, after Keith's death, Delia never sang again. If he was disappointed by the outcome of his efforts, Derek never showed it through his words or his expressions. He continued to be as supportive of Delia as he had always been.

The clock in the hall struck one. Delia decided she would offer Mr Lawton some coffee; it was the least she could do. In the kitchen, she gathered two cups and saucers, two teaspoons, a sugar bowl, and a jug of milk, placing them all on a tray. She also prepared two measures of ground coffee in the cafetière and filled the kettle with water. Delia then returned to the lounge to wait for Mr Lawton arrival. Just as she was about to sit down, the doorbell rang. Was it Mr Lawton, arriving early?

Delia opened the front door to find a woman with blonde hair standing on the step. She looked younger than Delia. She tried to recall if she had seen her before. Just inside the garden gate, on the path, stood two young women. The woman on the doorstep spoke, "Hello, Mrs Brownlee. You probably don't remember me, but we have met. I was Derek's PA for a number of years. My name is Hazel Skilton. I know what I'm about to say will be a shock for you. Standing near the garden gate are Zoe, she's 20, and Claire, she's 18. They are mine and Derek's daughters. Derek often told me he would never leave his Delia. I loved him, even though I knew he would never be just mine. I hope you will invite us in. The solicitor, Mr Lawton, said we should come to you for the reading of my, no, our darling Derek's will."

A Question

He locked the front door and walked down the garden path, noticing that the garden was overgrown. He decided that he would get someone to come and sort it out in the spring. He closed the garden gate that had been left open by the paper-boy. He looked back at the house, it seemed really too large for him now. The sign on the wall next to the front door was faded but just discernible, reading 'Vicarage'. It was a damp and chilly evening, the last Advent Sunday before Christmas, the nativity season. Houses along Glebe Lane were nearly all lit up, adorned with decorations like fir trees with fairy lights and tinsel. He remembered walking hand in hand through the fields on either side of the lane when they had come to see the Vicarage for the first time.

He turned right onto Church Road, passing houses adorned with decorations. The row of shops, the bakers and butchers, also had their lights on, and signs in their windows wished Merry Christmas and Seasons Greetings. Larns Chemist displayed the same small artificial tree in the window a tradition that had continued for many years. In the sub Post Office window, there were toys, jigsaw puzzles, and children's books on display, accompanied by a sign advertising reduced prices. It was Christmas Eve, a Tuesday, and they were hoping for further sales, as commercialism often overriding the message of the nativity.

No one was about; everyone was indoors, except for one man in the distance walking his dog. He pulled his overcoat collar up near to his ears. It seemed to him that he noticed the cold more now than he had in previous years.

The Town Hall clock struck five as he walked through the lynch gate and along the path to the church. On either side of the path grave stones, some dating back more than four hundred years. There were no funerals here now except for the wife or husband of a spouse buried here previously. He could see the top of his wife's gravestone. The flowers in the vase must be dead due to a sharp frost last night. A memory came to him, kneeling at the side of her grave as her coffin was lowered into the ground, relatives and friends standing around. A curate, who was with him at that time, intoning the words he had so often spoken himself: "Man that is born of woman hath but a short time to live." He sighed and walked on. The wreath he had ordered should arrive tomorrow. He would bring it to her grave straight away and remove the dead flowers, then pray for her again and spend time by her grave.

In the church porch, he noticed parish notices on the left board, some of them were out of date. He thought he must remove them later. The aged oak door opened easily on its well-oiled hinges. He descended two steps, walked four paces, and stopped. To his left were two shelves with hymn books, psalters, and other service books used from time to time. After two more paces, he stopped again. On the left, he saw the font, which had been used twice for Christenings yesterday. Beyond the font, he noticed the ropes that rang the bells, hanging down. The peal of the bells so often heard before sung Eucharist at 11am. He turned and continued to walk down the nave, where plaques on the walls commemorate long-dead parishioners. He knew the names, dates, and dedications of them all and had long since ceased to look at them.

He reached the first pew on the left after three paces and sat down where she had sat so long ago. He remembered looking down at her smiling face when he delivered his sermons from the pulpit. He knelt on a hassock, bowed his head, and said a prayer for her soul, her spirit, believing that it continued to exist Even though her body turned to dust so many years ago. He sat up again, reminiscing more about her in the church and the Vicarage garden. She had been so full of energy and enthusiasm to assist him in his vocation. They had hosted parishioners, organised parish events, and run the Sunday school together. Her faith and commitment to God were as deep within her as within himself. Their hopes of having a family, ideally a girl and a boy, had gone unfulfilled. He looked at the chancel, the choir stalls on either side, and the organ, with echoes of hymns, psalms, and prayers sung and chanted over many years playing in his head.

The altar and the sanctuary were a familiar sight. The altar was covered with a lace cloth, Adorned with a vase of flowers and two candles on either side of the crucifix. A memory that always returned was their wedding day, such a happy time in this church.

Now, he said out loud, a statement of fact and posing a question, "Lord, I have served you faithfully in this church and parish for fifty years to the day. My wife died after only three years and two months of marriage. The reason you had it so to be was a test for me?"

The silence in the church was slightly disturbed by the sound of birds on the roof.

The verger, standing just inside the church door, heard the question asked, as he had on many Sundays in the past. Now, what was, in fact, a routine, would unfold. The vicar, his good friend of nearly thirty years, would sit for a moment or two to gather his thoughts. He would take seven paces, stop at the step to the chancel and bow his head. At that point, the verger would switch on the lights, light the altar candles, ready for evensong. He would then go to the vestry to see his friend, a friend who had brought a change in him. He was an agnostic who accompanied his wife to church and, over time, had come to believe. His friend's ability to clarify, and where necessary to simplify the message for people, was always in evidence. Services here were always well-attended, whereas congregations dwindled elsewhere. Time would pass before the members of the choir and the congregation started to arrive.

At first, the routine seemed to be as usual. His friend bowed his head. Suddenly, the gloom in the church was gone. A bright light, not the result of pressing a switch, lit up the church. The light streamed through the stained glass window above the altar. The verger trembled and leaned on the wall. In the light over the altar, a figure dressed in white, a smiling young woman with her arms held out before her, appeared.

The verger heard his friend, now on his knees, say, "My dearest, my darling, you have come for me." The form of a younger man floated up and into the outstretched arms of the woman.

The light and the vision faded away. Only light from the alter candles, not lit by a match, showed the body of the vicar of All Saints prostrate on the floor of the chancel.

The verger leaned on the back of a pew, still trembling. He knew his friend's question had been answered at last, and he was now reunited with his wife after all those years apart.

A Conundrum

"Lionel, it's you." "Yes, Anna, it's me. After all these years, we meet in a hotel in Spain. I would like to think it was fate, Anna, however, I arrived yesterday with my wife and three children. The oldest one is ten. We flew from Stansted and are here for two weeks."

"The same for us, two weeks, Lionel. My husband and our two children, our eldest is also ten. We flew from Luton." "So, it's about thirteen years since we last met, my one-time girlfriend. Unlucky for some, thirteen."

"Lionel, I waited for you outside the Gaumont cinema for just about an hour. I arrived there at six, expecting you would be waiting for me. You were always early, never late."

"Anna, I arrived there just before seven. Which one of us got the time wrong, moot point? We must have missed each other by minutes. This sounds like the old joke. He waited at Kings Cross, and she waited at St Pancras. They met forty years later on platform two at Euston. Come on, Anna, if we don't laugh, we will cry."

"Yes, it's funny, Lionel, and you are right, spilt milk, I suppose. At first, I thought you had stood me up after being together for two years. I cried that night. I then thought something might have happened to you. Your dad had retired early and left with your mum to live on the Lincolnshire coast. I had no address for the guest house you were living in. The office where you had worked just said you had left and would not say more."

"Similar thing for me, Anna. Yes, I wept over you. Your family was between houses, and I had no address. Your old firm said you had got a new job and left. That was it, no trace of you. I did tell you I had applied to join the RAF. I was accepted, and I was going to tell you that evening. After basic training, I was selected for the RAF College at Cranwell and trained as a pilot."

"You flew planes, what sort?"

"As a pilot officer, I was with a fighter squadron. The last one I flew is still in service, the Eurofighter Typhoon. I now fly a mahogany bomber."

"A what?"

"I sit at a desk; my rank is Squadron Leader, call it an admin post. I got married, and I love family life. What happened to you, Anna?"

"I met my husband at the firm I was working for. He is a senior engineer and is very well paid. Like you. I love family life."

"My wife and kids are down by the pool. I have just been for a haircut, so no rush to get back. I might have had to wait. How about you, Anna?"

"No rush, I have had a trim, would you believe. I might have had to wait as well. My husband and our two kids are also at the pool."

"Let's walk along here and through the garden, it's the long way round to the pool. OK with you, Anna?"

"No problem, you soon found your way around."

"I have navigated aircraft half way around the world. It would be a bit much if I got lost here."

"You are showing off, Mr. Squadron Leader, but that's you, as I remember you, easy to get on with and full of jokes."

"I have thought of you from time to time, Anna. Believe it or not, often in a fighter, flying at twenty to thirty thousand feet on a long flight when the plane essentially looks after itself."

"I have thought of you, Lionel. Don't laugh, it's when I'm doing the ironing or washing up. You're laughing!"

"Yes, I was thinking of you when travelling at high speed, thousands of feet up in the sky. You are up to your elbows in fairy liquid bubbles or doing a neat job on your smalls when you have thought of me."

"Alright, it is funny. Have you got a tissue?"

"Seriously though, Anna, I'm very fond of my wife; she is very nice. She is always there for me with open arms if I have had to spend time overseas. We agreed as a family we would not move about, particularly when our children started school. Although, two years in Cyprus before schools were a concern was very nice."

"Lionel, the same as you, my life is good. My husband is always at home after work, and he is very good at helping around the house. He's very good with the children, and he always thinks of me. On Fridays, he often brings me flowers or chocolates. So while we are here, I think you and I should not let on we knew each other."

"Anna, I could not agree more. No doubt there will be contact in passing, hello, nice day that sort of thing. But I will say, my dear Anna, I will now have another pleasant memory of you."

"Yes, Lionel, I feel the same way. In a magazine called 'The World of Women', there was an article that you could say relates to you and me. It said if a first love is not carried through into the future, a residue of it will always be there at the back of people's minds, and that is us!" "My wife takes that magazine."

"Lionel, not only are you holding my hand, you have your other arm around my waist. So hold me tightly, another memory."

"Oh, Anna, I will do better than what you ask, kiss me please. An even better memory for both of us." "That was lovely, just as I remember you kissing me. But, come on, Lionel, back to sanity and formality."

"OK, Anna, we must think about my wife, your husband, and our children. Let's look through the bushes, and we can point out each other's partners. I can see our three in the shallow end of the pool playing with two others. They are throwing a ball to each other."

"Those two are ours, Lionel; they've made friends. That could make things a little more difficult. My husband is over by the shower; he is talking to someone."

"That's my wife, and they are holding hands. Anna, they have taken things further. I have twenty-twenty vision, but you can see as well as I: your husband is kissing my wife! Our children are watching them! They must, like us, have known each other in the past. They may make the same high-minded decisions about contact like you and me. But, my darling Anna, it's not as easy as that now. Oh, my darling Anna, kiss me again, and then we will go and talk to them and try and sort out this situation."

"If this situation was in a story, Lionel, there would be an epilogue in which it would all work out happily ever after."

"No epilogue, my lovely Anna, what we have here is a conundrum!"

The Song

"I'm home; I will pop upstairs for a quick wash and change. I can't wait to get out of this suit, collar, and tie. But before that, I will head into the lounge and see, as the yanks say, munchkin. More cartoons on TV? If you are not in the mood for talking, never mind. After tea and your bath, we'll have another bedtime story."

"I feel better now. As usual, I will set the table and empty the dishwasher. We will need some vinegar for the chips. Hey, Mrs, your cat wants to go out; there you go, puss. Now, the dishwasher. Did anything happen during your half-day at work?"

"Not really, the job's routine. I did have an ongoing conversation with Jade; she sits at the desk next to mine." "Oh yes, Jade of the glade, she was called by the lads at the school I attended. Many an adolescent lad was introduced to pleasures by Jade, which he had only talked or read about." "Not me, I hasten to add. I do know that, dear. Although it did take you until our first year at University to notice I was there; you were too busy with football, rugby, and other sports." "Alright, tell me more about what Jade had to say." "She said her husband developed what she called the seven-year itch." "More like ten in his case. Edwin Messenger married her when they were both sixteen, a shotgun wedding. We called him 'Headwind', get it?" "Yes, carry on." "Headwind told me and others that on his first date with Jade, he got to Boots to make a purchase just after they had closed. We all laughed, especially those who knew Jade better than Headwind. Back to the itch, tell me more."

"It seems every Saturday afternoon he goes out early and comes back late in the evening. He says he is going to a football or rugby match with a pal. On Sundays, it's fishing on the canal with the same pal. Jade bumped into the wife of this pal. She told her that they, along with their two children, had spent two nights the previous weekend at a small hotel on the coast. The following Saturday, Jade followed Headwind in her car. No football match; he picked up a young woman and drove out of town. On Sunday, it was fishing again, he said. Near the canal, yes, in a glade among the trees." "Probably the same glade we joked Jade rented when she was fourteen to sixteen. Any more from her?" "Yes, she told me, with glee, that she had seen you on three occasions when out shopping at lunchtime. Once with what she called a peroxide blond, another young woman, and an older woman, heavily made up. So, I think you know what she was inferring. Oh, she also said she is meeting someone else and was going to show Headwind the door in a month or so."

"That will be a blow for Headwind, and that's the dishwasher emptied. A blow, did you get it?" "Yes, I did. Now, can you start washing up the pans? It will save time later." "Right, now I will tell you about Jade seeing me."

"My HR manager job, as you know, involves vacancy advertising, arranging interviews with departmental managers, implementing legislation, and the firm's welfare policy. Elf and safety takes up a lot of time." "You've told me all this before, dear. Get to the point." "Okay, there is also a social work side to the job. Some might say it's beyond their remit with regard to the firm. I don't say so. The blonde I remember, she still works in the light products department. A Friday night out, too much to drink, and a bloke, who said his name was Joe, not seen before or since—pregnant. One lunchtime, I took her to see a doctor regarding her situation. She took three days of holiday to have an abortion on the NHS fund. There was another young woman, aged twenty, working in the Order and Invoice office with a regular boyfriend, and talk of engagement—pregnant. However, he refused to acknowledge her pregnancy and distanced himself. I made two lunchtime trips for her. The first one was to see her parents, a deeply religious family, with a crucifix on the hall wall, a painting of Christ over the fireplace, and a plaster statue of the Virgin Mary on the mantelpiece. To them, a baby is a gift from God. Fast forward, she went on maternity leave, and her parents provided childcare when she returned to work. The second lunchtime trip was to see the one-time boyfriend and tell him of his financial obligations towards the child when it is born. He called me an interfering son of a fucking bitch and attempted to attack me so I deck him. As there were no witnesses, I told him to cough up or I would be around to see him again." "Is tea nearly ready?" "Okay, one more story. There was an older lady on a production line who often wore makeup. She was a lead hand, and I talked to her about training courses as part of the job, and the possibilities of promotion. Unfortunately, it was not possible for her. Her main issue was her husband, who had been a drunken and verbally abusive presence in her life for years. Her two children were frightened to death of him. He started to get physically abusive. She even showed me a bruise on her arm. Fast forward again, the two children are now living with her parents, while she spends four nights in a hostel. She takes her meals in the canteen and spends weekends with her kids and parents. Is tea ready? Alright, I will go get our munchkin. And yes, I will stop saying that before you ask. Maybe I should look it up on Google."

"Bedtime story, goodnight kisses, and our little darling fell asleep straight away. Nursery school in the morning keeps her busy and tires her out. Regarding what I mentioned earlier about the social side of the job, it's where I get more satisfaction out of that than anything else. I was going to tell you all this when we had our two-day getaway. Your mum and dad are here to look after, I won't say it. I would like to take up a social work post, based on my degree and some experience I have been told I would be accepted for. It might mean less money to start with, but I could get another relevant qualification part-time, and then things should improve money wise. What do you think?"

"If that's what you really want to do, go ahead. I'm back at work now, so that will help financially."

"Come over here and sit with me on the settee. Now, what did you tell Jade with regard to what she was hinting at?"

"I told her she was wrong. As the song by Abba goes, 'I have faith in you'."

Alone

It's another Boxing Day, and the usual routine unfolds. I say hello as family arrives. My wife continues to chat, as I serve cups of coffee and drinks to the kids. Next, I go make a round with warm mince pies and cakes. They are all so busy in conversations, talking at and over each other, that I might as well be one of the ghosts from Dickens' 'A Christmas Carol'. Finally, I sit on a stand chair by the window, and at last, I'm included in the conversation. There's a request for more coffee and mince pies. I take a moment to mention, "I made the mince pies." However, there is not a dicky bird of response from my wife, her two brothers, or their wives. I can already predict that next year, it'll probably be mince pies from Mr Kipling or the Co-op, and I'm sure those will be commented on. I will not be baking; I'm not planning on being here.

I'm well aware why I get a back seat in family gatherings. My two brothers-in-law are successful professionals, earning over 100k+ a year in banking, finance, and various other business interests. They are both full of energy and drive, while I'm different, more serious and quiet to a point. My passion comes alive when I'm teaching my subject, which is English Literature at a sixth form college. Unfortunately, this profession does not cut the mustard with my wife, her brothers or their wives. Her brothers probably see me as a drain on the public purse, and the reason why they think they are paying too much tax. Their kids attend private schools. I have seen the writings of Dickens at one of their houses, and the works of Shakespeare at the other—purely for show, not for reading or enjoyment. Watching our two and our four nephews and nieces playing with the toys they have had for Christmas, I will be told again later: what we have bought our two is not as good as theirs. I have, more than once, been told by the same sister-in-law of my wife that we only live in this house because of what my wife inherited from my skinflint father-in-law. Though it was not directly said, but in a snide remark, which makes it abundantly clear that I do not earn anywhere near my wife's brothers' incomes. Nonetheless, I choose to let it pass; I don't care. Now, during mid-morning drinks, I serve up glasses of Prosecco and other drinks to the children. Unfortunately, one glass of coke ends up spilling. I can't help but wonder if there is anyone else who knows where the kitchen is to get a sodding cloth? Conversations soon shift to what has been achieved in annual bonuses by, you know who. Yes, both of them. I mention that I had a win on the Euro Lottery. A question was asked as to whether it was a mere ten pounds or my money back. Needless to say there was no chance they would believe that I actually won forty-four million quid. If that kind of wealth doesn't pique their interest, or even my wife's, then so be it.

It's present time again, another year, and I say thank you with a smile. However, it's as if I might as well have kept my mouth shut, for all the notice that's taken of me. One gift, a book about Shinto Temples and Shrines in Japan, presents thrilling reading material, probably bought for a pound from the clearance table at Waterstones. Another book I receive is titled 'Rough Shooting on Common Land' which sounds wonderful, except it requires a twelve-gauge or four-ten shotgun. The only thing I have fired is a Lee Enfield 303, stamped 1937, on a firing range when I was in the school cadet force. Unfortunately, five rounds rapid from that rifle would not be of much use for shooting pheasants or grouse.

Time to prepare Boxing Day lunch, so I head back into the kitchen. My dear wife offers some assistance but, after asking if I'm alright, rushes out to socialise. I serve lunch with a little help, but any thanks seem to have gone out of fashion. I sit down last and start eating my first course whilst everyone else helps themselves to dessert from the trolley I wheeled in. A choice of dessert for me? Forget it. All that's left is green jelly in the shape of a rabbit, and I made that! Cheese and port? I am about to take the last of the Brie when I receive a black look from my dear wife. She, the queen of snide remarks, takes the Brie with a superior smile. Bitch. So, I settle for a cheddar cheese slice, which I had bought for snide bitch's fussy son. More coffee, and this time I get some help from our eldest daughter. Now the kids are watching a Disney film on TV, and the adults are playing cards. I don't join in, as there have been grumbles in the past every time I win. But there's no admission though that I'm smarter at cards than any of them.

So, the dishwasher will have to be run at least twice. I wash up the pans and kitchen tools while wiping down the surfaces. It keeps me out of the way, but honestly, I've had it up to the neck. Boxing Day is always the same.

So, I announce that I'm going out to get some fresh air and smoke one of the cigars that snide bitch gave me for Christmas. Cigars? My arse, they're more like brown fags. Not a monkeys given as I leave the lounge.

It's chilly, damp and dark outside, but I don't care; being alone is enough. Alone? It seems to me I'm alone every day at home these days. My wife is always involved in managing the dress shop one of her brothers owns. Commission, commission, that's all she seem to think and talk about. Our two kids now have their own interests and friends, which no longer include me. I turn the corner onto the road I've lived on for what seems like an eternity and head to the High Street. I look at the BMWs displayed at the dealership. My old Fiat jalopy can get its coat on; a BMW 520D for me next. It will surely upstage my dear wife in her three-year-old Merc sports car, bought with a loan and her expectation of commission.

Shops are all lit up and closed, and there's nobody about. It's good because it suits my mood. Oh, someone has just turned the corner of Park Road. There is other life out and about. It's a woman, and I know who it is. I'm delighted to see her.

"Muriel, darling, how's Boxing Day been for you so far?" "Hello, Simon. I'm bloody well brassed off, to tell you the truth. His three brothers, their wives, and kids. For me, it's prepare this and that, serving food, drinks, nuts, dates, and bloody crisps. Preparing and serving lunch. After that, clearing up and loading the dishwasher. Doing other washing up and wiping clean the kitchen surfaces. Christmas Day presents for me? It's boxes of chocolates again. Today, how much talcum powder, shower gel, and shampoo do they think

I need? How it was for you, Simon, if that's the correct way to put it?"

"Same club as you, Muriel. Fucked off does not come close enough. No doubt, like myself, you made the excuse of needing fresh air to get away from it all." "Snap on that one, Simon. I sometimes wonder why I married him. I think having necked a bottle of Chardonnay made it seem like a good idea at the time. I said yes. It was fine at first, and I love our two kids. He is all about further expanding his building firm. It's totally fine, but when I mention teaching Geography, it does not get a look in during our conversation." "Similar thing happened to me, Muriel. Shop commission is fine, but when it comes to English Lit, forget about it. I must have asked her to marry me when there was a lull in the conversation. The truth is, I have plans, Muriel." "Tell me first, Simon, did you apply for the assistant head's job?" "No way, Muriel. We all know who will get that position. She sits at the front during staff meetings in her short skirts with her legs on display. Our head guru has his eyes on them all the time. It goes further than that, Muriel. I took some papers out to him at the last meeting, and there she sat with her legs apart. What she was offering him was winking at me." "I'm not surprised, Simon. Oh, Simon, if we had only kept in touch when we went to different universities." "I must admit, Muriel, that fresher's week for me was a big distraction. It was like being at a bargain basement sale. So were the next three years. How about you?" "I got a strained wrist from slapping faces and proving that a metal comb has more uses than one. But teaching at the same sixth form college has brought us together again. We're two people who were once very attracted to each other."

"Once, Muriel? Come on, eight times in the stationery cupboard and being your back-up on weekend Geography field trips for two nights." "That's true, Simon, naughty but nice." "Fess up, Muriel, it's called adultery." "True again, Simon, and I don't care the way things have turned out. However, we both agreed we could not upset our respective apple carts, children to consider. Oh, Simon, I wish we could turn our carts over. It's always good when I'm with you. I feel alive again, and I know you feel the same way; you have said so. There are times, like today, when I feel so alone."

"Agreed, Muriel, alone, out on a limb, so to speak." "What are the plans you mentioned, Simon?" "I was going to tell you at our so-called staff meeting the day after tomorrow. Sod event nine in the stationery cupboard. I will tell you now. I won forty-four million quid on the lottery." "That's a fortune, Simon." "True, the money's invested, and there's plenty of cash earning interest with easy access." "Wait a minute, Simon, do you smell smoke?" "Yes, look, it's coming from the far-end shop. That's the one she manages for her brother. Her commission is going up in flames." "It's more than that, Simon. His offices are on the two floors above. Expansion is going on hold, contraction more like." "Let's walk quickly on to the telephone box and make four calls, Muriel. Call the fire brigade, book a suite at the Plaza Hotel for you and I to live in, and tell him and her they can get their own evening snacks and drinks. Let the fire service tell them about the shop and offices. It will give them both something else to think about other than necking booze and stuffing their faces."

"Slow down, Simon, but I do like what you are saying. The Plaza Hotel, a suite, more than just a bedroom. I don't need a nightdress if I'm in bed with you." "We can buy new clothes tomorrow, Muriel, no problem." "Please hold me close and kiss me Simon." "Hang on, wait until we get to the telephone box; it will be warmer in there." "Carry on with what you were saying, Simon, I can wait."

"Tomorrow we will speak to them about a divorce, admitting adultery will do the trick. Offer them one mil each and only pay over slowly so we have access to the kids. Also, we can put money on one side for our children. You and I can do the decent thing and work a term's notice and then travel the world. See countries you have only ever talked about. After that, if we wish, get a teaching post in private school and do the thing we both enjoy—teach. Longer holidays, plenty of time to enjoy life and no money worries. What do you say to that, my lovely Muriel?"

"Yes, and ninety-nine time more, yes, my darling Simon. Together, you and I will never again feel, especially on Boxing Day, alone."

Two Letters

Len locked the garage door and looked at the front garden, leaves blown by the wind were scattered across the lawn and driveway. He opened the front door and quickly went in. As he closed the door, he called, "I'm home, and I've taken Friday afternoon off. The wind is knocking the daffodils and tulips about." There was no reply. He hung up his coat in the hall cupboard and walked down the hall into the kitchen, which was neat and tidy as usual. Len assumed that Leanne had probably gone to the corner shop. A Waitrose delivery this morning, so maybe she had forgotten something she wanted and decided to make a quick trip after sending her order online. He knew that she had spent two evenings carefully putting the items on the order.

Len noticed an envelope on the kitchen table. He thought it could be a note about her mother. She had mentioned that her mum seemed okay yesterday, but at eighty-six, who knows? He decided to have a mug of coffee first and then read it. There was only enough coffee for him in the container; perhaps it was coffee that she had missed? Len sat down at the kitchen table, the coffee still too hot to drink. He picked the envelope up and noticed his name, Leonard, on the front. He wondered when was the last time Leanne had called him

Leonard or written it. Len opened the envelope and found two pages from a writing pad, not the usual paper from the pad on the hall table. His name, Leonard, appeared again. Tension building, he held his breath and read on:

"Leonard,

Life for me has changed. Just over two weeks ago, when I visited Mum, someone I knew in the past was visiting his father. He had been my boyfriend for over twelve months. He was offered a well-paid job in Canada and asked me to marry him and go there to live with him. I was just eighteen, and he was twenty-three. My mum and dad were against me marrying and going, saying I was too young to make such a big decision.

Before he left, he asked me to consider joining him and marrying him later. We wrote to each other for nine months. I met you and stopped writing to him. He got married, and he has two sons; his wife died two years ago. He told me on a previous visit to see his mother and father, his wife was with him, he saw you and me walking in the park. He was still attracted to me. He told me that it had been over a year after I told him in my last letter I would not write again, before he went out with anyone else. His wife looked more than a little like me; he showed me a photograph of her. He said she was always happy but did not realise that when he was with her, part of his mind was with me. She was, in fact, in place of me.

We have been seeing each other every day, and he has asked me again to marry him. I have said yes, so this will mean you and I will need to get a divorce.

I will not be returning to you; I'm going to stay with him at his mother and father's home. We will be leaving to go to Canada in just over three weeks, so there are things to do and arrangements to be made. You will need a solicitor. I have already been seeing one, and I was told grounds of desertion would suffice from your point of view. I will come to the house the day after tomorrow to talk to you. My lovely man says he will come with me to support me. I shall get more of my clothes and other things I would like to keep.

The twins will return, as you know, for the Easter holidays next weekend. I will talk to them, and yes, it will be a shock for them. It is their third year at university, and I think they are old enough now to get over it and get on with their lives. You can be with me then, if you wish, or talk to them later after I have left.

To say sorry, I'm well aware that it will mean nothing to you. During our married life, you have been a very nice man. Leanne."

Len felt a mixture of rage and a feeling akin to grief, and yes, his love of Leanne churning inside him. In near disbelief, he read Leanne's letter again. He got a packet of cigarettes out of his pocket, selected one, and lit it. It was the first time he had lit a cigarette in the house since the day he and Leanne moved in. Len sat, smoked, his mix of emotions ebbed and flowed. He put the cigarette out on the surface of the kitchen table.

He picked up the mug of coffee and threw it across the kitchen. The mug hit a kitchen unit; broken pieces fell onto the granite work surface and the tiled floor. Coffee ran down the unit onto the work surface and onto the floor. He threw the condiment rack at the mug tree. They fell onto the floor and the broken pieces scattered everywhere.

Len got up, looked at the letter, and shouted, "I love you, Leanne, you lousy fucking bitch. How could you do this to me?" He walked into the hall. There was a vase on the hall table she had always liked; he had bought it for her. Len picked it up and threw it at the hall mirror. The vase and the mirror shattered. Mirror glass and pieces of the vase scattered over the hall table and onto the carpet. "Seven years bad luck now, you bitch," he shouted. Len lit another cigarette and walked on the broken glass into the lounge. On the sideboard was an ornamental dish, bought as a souvenir of their honeymoon in Greece. He tapped cigarette ash into it. On the same wall as the sideboard was their wedding photograph. Len looked at it; he was in uniform. He shouted, "When I married you, you lousy fucking cheating cow, I had just been promoted to Warrant Officer and was two weeks away from signing on again. I did not sign on because I loved you, and I had no wish to go back to being the man I had been as a soldier. I love you, Leanne. I've always been true to you. I have never been so with other women," the thought crossed his mind. "Oh, Leanne, Leanne, please don't go, don't leave me."

Two names came back to him. He had treated them badly, vague promises of engagement or marriage to get his way with them. He had left without giving an address when his leave ended. There were other women as well, nameless now. "Poetic justice, some might say you are doing this to me," Len shouted. "Oh God, I do so love you, Leanne." Sadness was turning to rage, love was nearing hate.

On the sideboard, next to the ornamental dish, there was a tulip in a small glass vase. He had brought it in the day before, the stalk was broken. He looked at it and remembered how Leanne had just taken it from him, got the small vase, and put the tulip in it without saying a word. Other signs of what was coming began to flood his mind. Lean going to bed early, claiming to be tired. Pretending to be asleep or actually falling asleep when he got into bed. Keeping herself busy with household chores, whether in the kitchen, the utility room, or somewhere else in the house. Yes, the bloody Waitrose order was just an excuse anything to avoid spending evenings with him. His temper flared, the pain of his feelings, and his love for her all culminated in a shout, "I won't live without you." He picked up the glass vase and threw it at their wedding photograph. The shards of glass fell onto the sideboard and lounge carpet. The cigarette, still lit, dropped into the ornamental dish. Smoke lazily spiralled upwards. Len opened the drinks cupboard, found only a little whisky left, drank it from the bottle and threw the bottle at the TV screen.

Len took the stairs two at a time, turned left on the landing, and went into the room he used as an office. He sometimes worked from home. He settled into the office chair that Leanne had bought him one Christmas, saying, "It's better for your posture, dear." "So much for your bloody concern," he shouted. On the desk, there were copies of business papers, pens, pencils, and three holiday brochures. The top brochure was about rail holidays in Canada. With a shout of 'Fuck' Len swept everything off the desk with his left arm. On the window sill, two photographs: one of his mother and father, and the other one of himself and Leanne, both smiling and holding hands. He looked at the photograph of them together for a few minutes.

Len opened the bottom drawer of his desk, removed two folders of paperwork, and took a short bayonet from the drawer. He put the bayonet on the desk in front of him and stared at it. It was not a souvenir; it was a reminder of the soldier he had been and what he had done. These Images sometimes appeared in his dreams, waking him up drenched in sweat. Leanne did not know about them; she had always slept peacefully beside him.. The image of a man in his ragged uniform running towards him, a rifle and bayonet held out before him, fear written in his eyes and on his face. He sidestepped, grabbed the man's rifle, and jerked it hard to the left. The man lost his hold on the rifle and his momentum carried him forward. He fell on his face and rolled on to his back. His halting words, pleading, echoed again. "No, no, wife, child." Len had used the man's own bayonet on him, a thrust to his chest and another into his throat. It was the killing of a man who, according to the so-called rules of war, should have been taken prisoner. The officer in charge, the boss, could have charged Len for murder, a war crime. But the boss had instead shot another wounded man who was trying to crawl away. Len remembered the boss's words again: "We do not want any witnesses to this action. Carry on." Other thoughts and missions from the past passed through Len's mind. Spain, too. A milestone of rage, temper, feelings of betrayal, entangled with love of Leanne, were no longer in evidence. Len was now in a detached state of mind, one that had often been required in his past to achieve an objective, whether with a knife or just his bare hands.

Len opened the middle drawer of his desk, and took out a pad of A4 paper. He picked up a pen off the floor and started to write.

"Dear Leanne Penelope,

Your letter to me has destroyed my life. You said I was a nice man, but as a soldier, I was much less than nice. I told you about Cyprus, Canada, where I trained once when we looked at the brochure on holidays there. The recent TV programme about the SAS you wanted to watch, and I pretended to read the evening paper. The truth is, I was in the SAS, and I was involved in that siege incident. You may remember what was said about what happened inside the building. It was mentioned on the programme. I did not want you to know anything about what I have been a part of, doing what I was ordered to do, was never a problem to me back then."

Len stopped writing, put down his pen, and reached to the back of the bottom drawer. He took out four presentation boxes. He opened them and put them at the back of the desk. Len looked at four medals. He picked the pen up and started to write again.

"There are four medals on my desk, each with a copy of a citation. They will say, in so many words, I was not a nice man. I have only gone back to being less than nice once whilst I have been married to you. You will remember our holiday with the twins, Malaga, Spain. The year they past the eleven plus, 2008, the last year the examination was held. A man bothered you, touched you from time to time. I said, 'Let it go; some men are like that.' He put both his hands on your bottom and tried to pull you to him and kiss you on the night of the flamenco show and dancing. He must have thought I had not seen him try it on. Enough was enough for me. You and the girls went up to our rooms at twelve. I stayed in the lounge to finish a drink and a cigarette, or so you thought. The next morning, he was found injured in the garden. Policia Local and the Guardia Civil were there. He had a broken jaw, broken arm, and damage to a sensitive part of his body, which was courtesy of me. A nice man?

When the house is sold, sorted out, and my share of what you and I have in terms of cash, bank accounts, and investments is known, please split my share between the girls. Everything is in our joint name; I always made certain of that.

Everything that needs to be done will fall on you. I will not need a solicitor. I will not, in fact, be here on Sunday when you come to what has been our home. If I was, I would not be able to stop myself from doing what I was very good at. He, him, whatever his name is, would have no need of an airline ticket to Canada. A nice man, you said in your letter, but I know more ways to kill someone with my bare hands than you could guess. If he is who you want to be with, so be it. I have no wish to live without you. I love you, Leanne, as much as I always have, in spite of your letter to me.

Goodbye, Leanne.

Len."

Len put his letter into an envelope, sealed it, and wrote on the front, 'Leanne Penelope'. He went downstairs and put the envelope on the kitchen table next to Leanne's letter to him.

He went back upstairs and sat again in his office chair. Len looked at the photograph of them both. He lit a cigarette, and thought of her. Later, he put the cigarette out in a box of paper clips in the top desk drawer, and picked up the bayonet. He placed the back of his left hand on the desk and put the point of the blade against his wrist, where he knew there is an artery. The blade of the bayonet was not very sharp and of no use for what he intended to do. It required brute force with a bayonet, and Len knew he would bleed out and end his life. There were other quicker ways. The voice still echoed in his head. "No, no, wife, child." He looked again at the photograph of himself and Leanne, took a deep breath, and was about to provide the force to push the bayonet through his wrist when he paused and said aloud, "No, no, my daughters."

He heard the front door open, followed by the sound of it closing. Leanne's voice reached his ears, "What a mess, who did this, and why?" The sound of her footsteps echoed through broken glass as she continued, "Oh, my kitchen, too." Her voice, no longer the sound of a house proud lady, was marked by shock. "Oh God, Len's been home, and he's read my bloody letter, and he's left one for me. Jesus, what have I done?" Now, silence hung in the air, as Len knew Leanne was reading his letter. He got up, went out onto the landing, and stopped at the top of the stairs. A minute passed before Leanne's voice, now raised in a shout, reached him, "Len, Len, where are you? What are you going to do? My darling, this is all my fucking fault!"

Len called out, "I'm here upstairs, and I'm coming down." As he reached the bottom of the stairs, Leanne rushed to him and put her arms around his neck. He put his left arm round her waist. "Hold me close, Len," she sobbed, but then she realised he only had one arm around her. Leanne looked down and saw the bayonet; he was still holding it in his right hand. Len dropped the bayonet on the floor and put his arm around Leanne's waist. For a minute or so, they stood with their arms around each other; nothing was said. Leanne kissed Len, and he kissed her back. "I'm so sorry, Len, for what I've done. I thought I would be back here before you got home from work in time to destroy that damn letter I wrote." "Let's sit in the lounge, Leanne, I'm afraid I've made a mess in there as well. I will help you to clear it all up later." They sat on the settee, and Len put his arm around Leanne's shoulders, holding her close to him.

"Len, my darling, I can't say sorry enough about what I've done. When I met him again, I felt like I was back in time, making a decision, saying yes, all in a whirl with a person I was once very fond of. Len, please believe me, nothing happened between us. Well, he held my hand, put his arms around me, and kissed me a number of times. I felt like an eighteen-year-old again, stupid, stupid me. After I had written that bloody letter in the kitchen, like some second-rate heroine who had found true love, I phoned him to come and collect me. He has a hire car. As I waited, reality started to dawn on me, and I asked myself, 'What are you doing?' I looked around my lovely kitchen, went into the lounge, and around the rest of the house. In one of the girl's bedrooms, I asked myself again, 'What the hell are you doing?' I should have told him when he arrived at the front door I was not going with him, that it was over. But I didn't. I sat in the car and looked at the house, and memories of you and our girls flooded into my head. I said nothing during the drive into town. He did not seem to notice and kept talking about Canada and the place where he lives, it's called Kamloops. He mentioned that the Rocky Mountaineer stops there overnight. That hit me hard; we had talked about a holiday travelling on that train. Again, I should have told him right then that I was not going with him. He was obviously happy and content that I was with him after all the years he had thought about me. It made it harder for me to open my mouth. He suggested that nice restaurant, The Harlequin, near the Town Hall for lunch. He kept talking. All I could managed was one-word answers and no other odd words. He did not seem to notice that I was not really with him. What finally gave me the courage, the resolve, to tell him was when he mentioned tonight. He said I had no need to worry about his mother; her room is next to ours, and she is quite deaf, she would not hear anything. He meant it as a joke. I realised he was assuming that I would be sleeping with him. That did it. The meal was served, and as he picked up his knife and fork, I stood up and said, 'I can't do this. I'm going back home to my husband.' I walked out and left him sitting there."

"Please, please forgive me, Len, I love you, only you." Len held Leanne close to him and kissed her. For minutes, nothing was said; they just held each other as if they never wanted to be apart again.

Len looked at Leanne, smiled, and said, "Give things a day or two, and I'm sure we can pick up again from where we were. We can put all this behind us. All I ask of you is to try and forget what I put in my letter. You now know more about me than I ever wanted you to. I hope you will again be able to think of me as the nice man you married and who loves you." Again, they kissed, and Leanne said, "Take me to bed, Len." He picked Leanne up and made his way through broken glass to the stairs.

The bond between them, for now, re-established. In the lounge and the hall, damage, a mess. In the kitchen, a mess, a burn mark on the table, and two letters. One saying, "I'm leaving you for someone else." The other saying, "You do not know me, what I've done, and what I am capable of."

The evening paper, put through the letter box, landed on the doormat. The headline—**CANADIAN VISITOR—SUICIDE NOTE.**

Implications:

A mother, eagerly anticipating her son's return with the lady, who he says is going to marry him, only to receive the devastating news of his tragic drowning.

A father in a care home, robbed of his ability to recognise the lady his son had a close relationship with when she visits the home to see her mother.

Two sons in Canada, expecting their father to return with his second wife, and are happy for him, only to be informed that he has taken his own life.

Two daughters, coming home for the holidays, will they notice a hint of tension between their mum and dad?

Len said, "Put all this behind us." Will their lives together in the future ever be quite the same as previously?

Intellect and Compatibility

"Good tea. Assam, I hope, and not the cheap brand you bought previously. I see you have baked your favourite Victoria sponge cake again. I have said previously that rich fruit cake should not be regarded as taboo. Today, as you know, I reached my forty-eighth year. Thank you for the card, the same as the one you gave me last year. Another cheap charity pack, I presume."

"I think the time has come for you and me to have a serious chat. The last thirty years of marriage to you have, overall, been fine. The attraction we shared for each other has lasted, well until about five years ago. When I suggested experimentation to rekindle the flame, you thought I was going to join an evening class to study chemistry. You seemed to have forgotten I have a degree in it, and I have been teaching the bloody subject for years!"

"We both played our part in bringing up our two sons, although they were awkward little buggers at times. To give you your due, you were far better at kicking and heading a ball than I or them. Casting a fly when fishing for trout, you are superb. Better than I or those lazy sods. Now they are independent of us and have, as they say, flown the nest. To be honest, if either one of them comes back in the next twelve months, it will be too damn soon."

"We share the same taste in comedy, to some extent. 'One Foot in the Grave', 'Open all Hours', and 'Only Fools and Horses'. Although 'Have I Got News for You' leaves you cold. To you, current affairs are about what film stars get up to. Music is a shared interest to a point. I have a wide appreciation, jazz through to grand opera. We both enjoy popular music, 'Queen', for example. What amazes me is that you have no appreciation of the sentiment in the words of a song. Even 'Knowing me, Knowing You' by Abba leaves you cold. You tap your foot and dance around. The words, to you, it seems, are just there to give singers a job. As for light opera, when I took you to see 'The Mikado' by Gilbert and Sullivan, you thought we would see Gilbert O'Sullivan. 'The Magic Flute' by Mozart is, to you, heavy stuff. I do think that about 'Wagner', say 'Gotterdammerung' for instance. No wonder Hitler liked it. Oh yes, 'Mozart', you thought 'Cosi Fan Tutti' was a new brand of ice cream. I nearly fainted when you asked for it in Tesco. A large paper bag over my head with holes cut in it so I could see it would have covered my embarrassment. The manager laughed his socks off when you told him you could guarantee that Sainsbury's would sell it."

"Film, shared taste to an extent, The Sound of Music is entertaining, I agree with you. However, you missed the point about Captain Von Trapp not wishing to be involved with the National Sozialistische Deutsche Arbeiterpartei. Alright, Nazis to you. The Matrix was a no-no, your brain could not grasp the complexities. There are TV soaps like Coronation Street and others, and I know you are an avid viewer. I tolerate it if the weather is poor and I'm unable to go out into the garden and smoke my pipe."

"We do have a shared interest in horticulture—gardening, I cannot fault you with regard to the lawn, you mow it on a regular basis. You are always enthusiastic when turning the vegetable plot over in the autumn. Also, you are very good at cutting the hedges. But, it does annoy me when you are unable to remember the correct names of plants. For example, Tulipa means tulip. You sodding well forget from one year to the next. And as for architecture, I mentioned the book about Greek Temples I was reading. You asked if Doric Columns was the author of the book and also if Doric was male or female. That led to exasperation. When you were up a ladder painting, you asked if art deco was a special way of using a paintbrush. I jokingly said that only professional decorators knew how to do it, and that stopped further discussion. I was just about to head down to the lounge to read my Saturday Guardian, putting your copy of the Sun aside, when you asked me to go to B and Q to buy more white emulsion. My Saturday morning was ruined due to your inability to plan ahead."

"Literature to you is Mills and Boon, or magazines about film and TV stars, so-called 'personalities'. Put the Three Sisters by Anton Chekhov in front of you, and you think it is in a foreign language. My copy is not printed in the original Russian. I could go on and on. I will say I don't look down on your tastes; for you and many people, Corry and low-brow books, etc., are all that you want or need, and you are happy with that. But when I compare your tastes to mine, they rarely coincide."

"My friend, whom I meet at the Book Club and the Music Appreciation Society, shares my tastes. We are not poles apart.

As you know, we have spent many happy hours at performances of the local opera society and the Shakespeare group. We have also taken trips to London, leave Friday evening and returning Sunday night, to see Swan Lake, Carmen, and other productions. My friend and I engage in in-depth discussions regarding the writings of Voltaire, Freud, Proust, Rousseau, and other writers. A discussion with you comes down to who is likely to shag who on Love Island, or will some so-called celebrity eat grubs on the TV show that I do not even care to name. One of them has now been a cabinet minister! At least she knew the price of milk."

"So the time has come for you and me to consider our future. To be candid, it comes down to this: I will divorce you on the grounds of incompatibility. You have heard me on the phone with my friend Chris, but Chris does not phone me. It's not Christopher, the one you met at a bridge club social evening; it's actually Christine. She is financially independent and a commercial artist in her own right. Christine is my soul mate, and our tastes coincide across the board. She has agreed to marry me once I'm free from you. I already know she is very flexible in her thinking with regard to intimacy. Above all, we are intellectual equals. Compatibility is thus assured."

"What are you doing? Cake, jam, icing sugar all over me. Get back; let me get up. That tea is hot; don't pour it on me there! For fuck's sake, put that bloody cake slice down!"

You

I was so nervous waiting to be interviewed.

I desperately needed to get another job. The firm I worked for was going to relocate fifty miles away. I could keep my job if I was willing to move. How could I? My dad was an invalid, and Mum was not well. Two other candidates sat talking; both of them seemed confident they would get the two jobs advertised. One of them glanced at me and said something; they both laughed. The waiting room door was open, and you were passing by. You stopped to talk to two ladies. That was it for me; my nervousness and nausea vanished. I wanted the job more than ever, so that I could be near you and see you every working day. After the interviews, we were asked to wait. Twenty minutes later, the HR manager told me I had got one of the jobs. At home, my mum and dad were delighted; I would not be moving away. After tea, my boyfriend from school days, who I was engaged to, called to see me. I suggested a walk. I told him I had got the job; he was pleased. On the corner of the street, I gave him his ring back and told him I going to see someone else. That was the last time I saw him.

I started work the following Monday, and you worked in the next office. Over the first two to three days, I saw you, but you did not seem to notice me. I was told by Mrs Green, who I worked with, that you were one of the golden boys who would succeed. She also said that you had dated a number of the girls from the offices. But, as Mrs Green put it, none of them had managed to reel you in. You first spoke to me when you visited the manager of the office I worked in, as you did from time to time, to talk to him. The manager called out, "Two cups of coffee, please." I was there like a shot, and you said thank you and smiled as I put the cups down on the desk.

From then on, when you saw me, you would say 'good morning' or 'hello' or 'how are you'. If you saw me at the bus stop, it would be 'goodnight' or 'have a good weekend'. Yes, everyday things that people say, but it pleased me so much. The festive season was the time it all happened for me. At the office party, everyone was happy and at ease. It was quite wild, as office parties can be. Girls and older women were getting men to join them under the mistletoe. You did not easily give in, and Mrs Green said, "You could have things all your own way and would play hard to get." I got up to get myself and Mrs Green a drink. As I walked to the bar, you got hold of my hand and said, "Join me under the mistletoe." I was in seventh heaven as you kissed me and held me tight. Mrs Green called out, "He's yours, hang onto him." I was with you for the rest of the evening. All my dreams had come true. You asked me to go out with you on Christmas Eve. I could not believe it; I was with you at last. On Boxing Day, you unexpectedly visited me at home. I introduced you to my mum and dad. We met each other every day between Christmas and New Year. We got married in the spring, and thanks to you having been promoted, we were able to buy our lovely house with its nice garden. It's still our nice home, and I am certain you would not wish to live anywhere else. We so loved each other, and we agreed that having a family would make our lives complete. I gave up work. You said a boy and a girl would be ideal. The bedroom next to ours, we prepared as a nursery. The wallpaper has nursery rhymes and the characters in them on it as well. The cot has a mobile over it, and the little one will sleep in it soon. The drawers in the chest are filled with baby clothes. Everything else we will need is ready and waiting. After my second miscarriage, the doctor told us to put that behind us; we still had plenty of time. We should relax when together and allow nature to take its course. With you, relaxing was not a problem for me. Life was as wonderful as it had been previously. We spent as much time together as we could, especially on our lovely holidays.

Alright, stop taking notes. She is repeating herself again. It's the second time we've heard this. "I have pages of notes, sir. The shorthand I learned after I left school has come into its own." "The witness to this, the postman, you said he was taken to the hospital?" "Yes, sir." He dialled 999. When PC Wendon and I arrived, he was in shock. He kept saying, "She is such a nice lady; we often had a chat." A paramedic passing by stopped. She said he would get over it and took him to the hospital so he could be kept in under observation. "We will get a statement from him later. Fine, you will have to help me with a report; I don't know a thing about shorthand. She is repeating herself again. We both tried to get her to talk to us. It's as if she is now in another world, occupied only by him and her. The doctor, or the ambulance crew when they arrive, might be able to get through to her. If nothing can be done about the state she is in, I think it is likely she will be sectioned under the Mental Health Act. She could spend the rest of her life talking to him, a CD on repeat. The baby will probably be put up for adoption." "It's sad, sir." "I thought after all my years on the force I was sufficiently detached, hard enough, to cope with all the situations we come across." "What got to me is her talking about time, the cot, and the little one." "She must be about two or so years past what is considered to be childbearing age." "People can get a surprise, as my sister and her husband found out." "Her husband must have thought she was letting herself go, putting on weight. What he said to her was just too much for her to take in. She thought she was fulfilling a hope, a dream that they both shared." "She probably had said nothing to him because of what happened to her years ago." "I shed a few tears." "I noticed." "The crime scene lot will have no need of fingerprints on the knife handle, as we have a witness." "He must have died instantly. The knife is in his chest up to the handle." "Sir, she is reaching the point where she mentions holidays." "What she says after that is critical with regard to the report." "I will listen again and check my notes." "Carry on if you must."

Lovely holidays. When I kissed you goodnight, as I always do, you told me you would be away on business today and would stay overnight in a hotel. I thought nothing of it. You had been doing this for over five months since you became a director of the firm. This morning I made your breakfast and then packed your overnight case. I got the car out of the garage for you, kissed you before you left and waved goodbye.

I decided to go into town to buy groceries and look around the shops. When I turned the corner near the Post Office, I saw you. You were greeting a young woman, you put your arms around her and kissed her. I caught a bus home and cried all the way. In our home, I thought I was wrong, it must have been another man. A Jaguar like ours was parked nearby; other people own those coloured maroon. I decided to partially prepare your favourite meal for when you returned home tomorrow evening. I was cutting up meat when I heard the front door open, and a moment later, you walked into the kitchen. You told me, "I know you saw me with her earlier. She is currently my secretary and travels with me on business. She is pregnant; it's my child. I will divorce you and marry her. I will be a daddy at last. Come into the lounge; we need to talk."

"I stopped cutting the meat and followed you into the lounge. You sat in your favourite armchair. I told you that you would never leave me. All the little one and I need to be happy, is to be with you."